Night Train

Night Train

JUDITH **CLARKE**

|||||||||||||||||||||

Coweeman Middle School
2000 Allen Street
Kelso, WA 98626

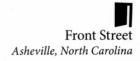

Front Street
Asheville, North Carolina

First published in the United States in 2000 by Henry Holt and Company
Originally published in Australia
in 1998 by Penguin Books Australia Ltd.

Library of Congress Cataloging-in-Publication Data
Clarke, Judith.
Night train / Judith Clarke. — 1st Front Street pbk. ed.
p. cm.
Summary: His family, peers, and teachers despair of
eighteen-year-old Luke, who seems to have turned himself
into a loser, failing at school, paralyzed with fear and
indecision, losing touch with reality.
ISBN 978-1-932425-92-5 (pbk. : alk. paper)
[1. Emotional problems—Fiction.
2. Family life—Australia—Fiction.
3. Interpersonal relations—Fiction.
4. Schools—Fiction. 5. Australia—Fiction.]
I. Title.
PZ7.C55365Ni 2007
[Fic]—dc22   2006101609

FRONT STREET
An Imprint of Boyds Mills Press, Inc.
815 Church Street
Honesdale, Pennsylvania 18431

For Heather

Into the Rain

Quickly, while Mrs. Richards was busy on the phone, Naomi seized her parka and slipped out through the back door into the rain.

They wouldn't let her see Lukie!

They'd told her Lukie had gone somewhere far away and none of them would see him for a long, long time.

That's what they'd said, but they'd been telling lies. Last night when she'd gone to the kitchen to get a glass of water she'd heard Mrs. Richards talking to her husband in the living room. Naomi had stood still in the hall and listened; she'd heard how Mum and Dad and Molly were going to see Lukie today. Uncle Ted and Auntie Maisie were going with them, and Auntie Irene too. Only Naomi wasn't allowed to go; they said she was too little.

Naomi knew the place where they were meeting Lukie: Fiorelli's, it was called. And it wasn't far away like they said, but just past the shops; a low grey building with wide stone steps and nothing in the windows and a bright green lawn all round. Sometimes there were big black shiny cars outside, all covered in flowers, and people in their best clothes crowded over the steps and lawn, like at a wedding.

"What's that place?" she'd asked her mum once and Mum had answered "Fiorelli's," and nothing more.

She knew how to get there; it was the way Mum drove to Kinder; you went down Mrs. Richards' street to the big road, up to the traffic lights, and then along the winding street towards the shops. It wasn't far, but it was further than she'd ever gone on her own before.

Naomi was getting wet.

The zip on her parka was stuck, but she didn't have time to fix it; she was scared Mrs. Richards would put down the phone and find she was missing and come after her. Turning the corner into the big road she felt safer, but now the wind caught her, ripping her hood back, and the cold rain soaked into her hair.

The grey sky was so low it seemed like you could reach right up and touch it; the road gleamed blackly, the gutters rushed and roared, the cars had their headlights shining in the middle of the morning.

Naomi ran and ran, but she had to stop at the traffic lights and wait till they turned green.

"Naomi!"

Naomi's head jerked up. A blue car had pulled up right beside her, and a lady was leaning out of it, holding the door open. Not Mrs. Richards, who had a green car, but one of the ladies from Kinder, Kelly Biber's mother. "Naomi, what are you doing here? Darling, you're soaking wet! Quick, get inside!"

No! Naomi forgot about the lights and ran straight out across the road, dodging the cars that hooted and shrieked and squealed all round her. She reached the other side and ran on again, her heart thudding in her chest, the blood beating loud in her ears.

Mrs. Biber would come after her, she knew. She'd turn her car round and follow; she'd jump out and chase her and take her back to Mrs. Richards. They'd stop her from seeing Lukie. Naomi turned the corner into the long winding road and darted through the gate of a tall white house with a grey paling fence. She had to hide. She crouched down behind the fence and peered through a narrow gap between the palings, waiting for the blue car to come round the corner.

And yes, there it was, moving slowly, with Mrs. Biber's frowning face peering through the window out onto the street. Naomi squeezed in close between the cold wet prickly bushes and held her breath. When the car had passed she stayed there, waiting, in case it came back again. And it did, but now the car was going faster and Mrs. Biber was just looking through the windscreen in an ordinary way. It turned the corner onto the highway and now there was nothing in the street except the rain.

Naomi scrambled out from the bushes, pulling her hood back over her dripping hair.

She had to hurry; she might be late, she might get to the place called Fiorelli's and find that Lukie had gone. She ran out the gate and up the long winding road. She ran and ran and ran.

West Chapel

It was called West Chapel, but it didn't look anything like a chapel, Molly thought. Just a big room with dark walls and polished floors and narrow windows so high up you couldn't see out of them—everything bathed in shadowless blue light. Someone had closed the doors and the chapel stank of wet wool and flowers and sweat and the sweet sick scent of air freshener.

The box—she wouldn't call it a coffin, she would never say that word—lay on a raised platform that was like a little stage. Dad stood beside it, stiff and straight in his best grey suit. Molly watched his eyes dip down inside the box and then away. "Margaret," he said to Mum, but Mum wouldn't look. "No, I don't want to!" she whispered, pulling away from his hand.

The chapel was crowded: Dad's friends from work and Mum's from the office, Auntie Maisie and Uncle Ted whom they hadn't seen since Christmas and Auntie Irene who'd come all the way from Wagga. There were kids and teachers from Luke's old schools; she saw Danny Pearson and Tom Griffin from Riversdale, and Mark Conlan from St. Crispin's. They were all right, because they'd once been mates of Luke's, and her boyfriend Lionel was all right because though he'd never met her brother, he'd admired him. But those other kids, all those kids from Glendale Secondary—they shouldn't be here; they shouldn't have been allowed to come. They weren't his friends, they probably hadn't even known him; they'd just come along to stare.

"Molly!" Her father was beckoning her over. She went and

stood beside him and looked down at her brother. She saw a boy with his eyes closed tight who didn't look the slightest bit like Luke. She'd have passed this boy in the street for a total stranger.

They'd done something to his face. It was like they'd taken all his features, his nose and mouth and brows and eyes, and arranged them in a different pattern, so you couldn't know him.

His hair! The hair made you want to weep. Luke's hair had been long and straggly and all over the place; this boy's hair was neatly combed and parted on the side. "Look what they've done!" she cried.

"What?" whispered her father in a frightened voice.

"Look what they've done to his hair!" Molly leaned over the box and put her hand inside; she rumpled the strange boy's hair, messing the parting, trying to make it look right. But the hair wouldn't go right, it just—fell, sliding through her fingers like limp cotton.

It felt funny, soft and cold.

"Molly, stop it!" Her father's hand grasped hers.

"Leave me alone!" Molly flung away from him and went to stand beside the wall. A blonde girl with wedges of dark shadow beneath her eyes came up to Molly and held out her hand. She was wearing the uniform of Glendale Secondary. "I'm Caroline," she said.

Molly nodded but didn't take the offered hand. She'd never seen the girl before; Luke had never mentioned anyone called Caroline.

The girl's hand dropped down by her side. "I'm sorry," she sobbed. "I'm so sorry."

Molly went back and stood beside the boy in the box. She leaned down to him. "Hi," she whispered. "It's me. It's Captain Coolibah."

He'd always called her that. She'd hated it.

"Luke, I didn't mean it," she said, "the way I was with you. I didn't mean any of it. You know I didn't, don't you? Don't you, Lukie?"

The strange boy just lay there. He looked like he didn't care about a thing.

A wild anger seized hold of Molly. "Why didn't you *say* something?" she cried at him. "Why didn't you *say*?" She kicked at the platform beneath the box. She kicked and kicked at it.

"Molly!" Her father caught her by the shoulders.

And then the door flew open.

Naomi was standing there.

A great hush filled the room.

"Where's Lukie?" cried Naomi, looking round and round.

No one answered her.

No one did anything, only—the crowd parted silently, leaving a narrow path between the doorway and the box. It was like that picture they'd had on the wall at Sunday school, thought Molly: Moses with his staff raised and the Red Sea falling back to let the Israelites cross over into Canaan.

Naomi ran along the narrow path because there was nowhere else to go. She stopped at the edge of the platform; she was just tall enough to look over the edge of the box and down inside. Molly watched her little sister's eyes dip down.

She didn't recognize him. Molly had known she wouldn't.

Naomi stared down at the strange boy in the box and frowned. Then she looked up again. Angry red blotches burned on her cheeks. Her cheated voice rang out accusingly. "Where's Lukie?" she demanded. "Where's Lukie gone?"

The Gazebo

Luke hurried across the Hamiltons' backyard towards the gazebo. The yard didn't belong to the Hamiltons now, of course, and he could see the changes all around: the trampoline gone, a vegetable garden along the back fence where Mrs. Hamilton's rosebushes had been, the lemon tree grown tall, fruit perched on its branches like fat yellow birds.

He'd been standing in the playground at lunchtime when the image of the old gazebo had slid suddenly into his mind. He hadn't thought of the place for years, he hadn't thought of Alex for years, even though Alex had been his best friend back in Primary School. The Hamiltons had moved to America when Luke was in Year 6, they'd probably have moved farther on by now; Mr. Hamilton had that travelling kind of job.

The windows of the gazebo winked at him, catching a sudden beam of sunlight. Gazebos didn't usually have windows, but this one did. Mrs. Hamilton had insisted on glassing in the open sides; winter in this town could be nine months long, she'd said, and she wanted somewhere for Alex and Luke to play where they wouldn't be under her feet.

"Somewhere to *hang out*," Alex had corrected her, protesting against the kiddy word. "Not *play*."

Mrs. Hamilton had laughed. "Hang out, then. A place for you both to hang out. Okay? Your special place."

Luke was on the step now. The door wouldn't open. He tugged and twisted at the handle but the thing refused to budge. Locked.

And he couldn't account for the strange panic that swept over him then, standing shut out on the step, a fierce hunted feeling as if something was after him and the gazebo was the only place left in the world to hide. He tore at the handle, thrusting the weight of his body against it; if that door didn't give he felt he might bang and kick at it, batter it down to get inside.

He didn't have to. The handle turned suddenly in his sweaty fingers and the door scraped inwards over a drift of old blown twigs and leaves. Luke blinked and stared round; he could see the place hadn't been used for years. Dust lay everywhere. Someone had taken down the curtains with the pattern of red racing cars; the straw matting had gone, leaving a floor of pocked and grimy concrete. He tossed his schoolbag down and sank into an old wicker chair. Across the road, the bell rang for sixth period.

Why had he come here? It was like his feet had just started walking of their own accord.

Sixth period was English with Ms. Brennan. There was no way he was going, even though he liked Ms. Brennan. She trusted him. "How's the Writing Folder going?" she'd asked him cheerfully last week, and there hadn't been the slightest hint of threat in her voice. "Okay," he'd answered, sounding cheerful himself, as if he didn't have a worry in the world. She'd think he was getting along fine with it; because hadn't he chosen poetry, Creative Writing 3B? She'd liked those poems he'd given her for the school magazine; she'd never imagine he'd have trouble with Creative Writing 3B. He couldn't bring himself to tell her what was really going on. He wasn't quite sure himself.

Luke's gaze slid downward to the bag he'd chucked there on the floor. Chucked. Sometimes a single word could bring things rushing back; and Dad's voice rushed in on him now, Dad's voice shouting, "You chuck everything back in our faces!"

Through the bag's open flap he could see the dog-eared corner of the blue folder crammed inside; he carried that folder round everywhere. He hadn't even made a start on it, not any start that you could see, even though he'd spent whole nights in his room clenched up to the desk, struggling to think of something. The Writing Folder was due in next Monday, less than four days away if you didn't count the weekend. It was worth thirty percent of the final English mark and already two kids had handed theirs in to Ms. Brennan.

Today there'd be some more, you could bet; kids who wanted to get it out of the way so they could start on their final revision. The tiny slap of those folders landing on Ms. Brennan's desk had sounded in Luke's ears like doors closing somewhere in a distant house.

Was that why he'd come here? Because he didn't want to hear that sound again, not till he'd finished it, not till he'd got the Writing Folder done? He stared down at the gritty floor, frowning. There were plenty of other places he could have bunked off English: the washroom, the sheltered spot behind the school canteen, the shed behind the boiler room. He could even have taken a stroll down to the shops. Why had he thought of the gazebo? And Alex?

He'd never found another best mate like Alex Hamilton. He'd had mates all right: Danny and Tom at Riversdale, Mark Conlan at St. Crispin's, kids he'd lost touch with since he'd come to Glendale Secondary, but he'd never really found anyone like Alex. They'd understood each other; they'd thought in the same kind of way.

Alex would be eighteen now, like him. He'd be in college somewhere, you could bet. He probably looked different. Luke himself had changed, he knew—whenever he looked at the old photo Mum kept on her dressing table, the one Dad had taken on the pier at Fairlie, he could hardly believe the stocky little blond kid with the great big grin on his face was actually him. It wasn't just the way he'd grown tall and skinny and his hair had darkened; he'd changed inside as well.

He'd been solid back then. Now he was all bits and pieces; worries and doubts and fears and little hopes all jumbled up together, like bits of a puzzle rattling round inside a box.

Luke yawned suddenly, rubbing at his eyes. He felt tired. He was always tired these days, sleepy in school and in the evenings when he was trying to work; but the moment he crawled into bed he started feeling wide awake. He yawned again and settled lower into the scratchy chair, leaning his head back, stretching his long legs out, getting comfortable.

It was lovely and warm in here with the sun shining in through the glass, lovely and warm and safe. The dusty wicker chairs clicked quietly, like tiny insects talking; the garden shone outside. Luke closed his eyes and concentrated, struggling to summon back the person he'd been all those years ago; he tried to *feel* the way that person had. It was why he'd come here, he realized suddenly. It must have been. If he could be solid, just for a moment, a single second, then he—

A tapping sounded at the window beside him, a short harsh tapping like an order drummed in Morse code.

Luke jumped, his eyes sprang open, he saw a face peering in at him. It wasn't Alex Hamilton's, of course, but it was a face Luke knew by heart all the same, a tense white face with narrow darting eyes.

It was the face of Clyde B. Stringer, the Deputy Principal of Glendale Secondary.

A Matter of Trespass

Clyde B. Stringer had lost all patience with students like Luke Leman; children who skipped classes, whose marks were unsatisfactory, who couldn't meet the standards.

They pulled the score down too; one bad failure in the HSC put the Glendale score back several places. Six years ago, Glendale had boasted the fourth highest pass rate in the state, two years back it had rated only twentieth, last year it had sunk to twenty-sixth.

He thumbed impatiently through Luke's bulging file, clicking his tongue occasionally, his small hard eyes swiveling from left to right. The boy shouldn't have been allowed to sit Year 12 again; he obviously couldn't be bothered to work. "You've got quite a record here," he said at last.

Luke didn't answer. His dad's voice came rushing through his head again: "Don't you *understand*, it's your record that people *see*?"

"What does the 'T' stand for?" Stringer asked him slyly.

"The 'T'?"

"Your middle initial."

"Thomas."

"I thought it might be 'T' for trouble."

Like yours is "B" for bastard, thought Luke angrily, but he kept the retort to himself. He fixed his gaze on Stringer's face; the waxy smoothness of it, the small black moustache which sat like a slug on his upper lip, the two round shiny knobs at his temples, as if Stringer might be about to sprout a pair of horns.

But Luke knew Stringer wasn't the Devil or anything like it; thirteen years of schooling had taught him to recognize the kind of person Stringer was: a loser who'd never make it to Principal, who'd stay a Deputy all his life. It was the losers you had to watch out for; back at St. Crispin's, Gosser had been a loser. But knowing this didn't help, because they had you in their net. Once you were past Year 10, people like Stringer knew you needed things, or your mum and dad needed them for you: a good pass in the HSC, a place at university, an entrance ticket to the world outside.

"Your luck's running out, isn't it, Leman?" said Stringer tauntingly.

Luke wanted to get up and leave. He wanted to spring from the chair, rush from the room, down the corridor, out through the playground into the street. But he stayed where he was; needing things made you into a coward.

"Because it was sheer luck I caught you in that house. Sheer luck I happened to be driving by." Stringer paused, steepling his fingers beneath his chin, gazing at Luke over the crest of his pink scrubbed nails. "I know the Mills family, you see."

Luke stared at him blankly. What was he talking about? Who were the Mills family? For a moment it crossed his mind that Mrs. Chambers had handed Stringer the wrong file; the file of some other kid whose second name was trouble too.

"The Mills family?" he echoed.

Stringer sighed wearily. "The people who live in the house you invaded."

Luke said quickly, "I didn't invade it. I didn't go into the house. I—"

Stringer brushed his words aside. "I serve on a committee with Mr. Mills, I know he has no children, so when I saw a boy in Glendale uniform creeping round the side of the house I knew he had no business to be there." His voice rose sharply. "And you *had* no business there, did you?"

Luke shrugged, and then Stringer dropped his bombshell. "By rights I should inform the police."

The bombshell had the effect the little man had intended. Luke was astounded, he couldn't keep the shock from showing on his face. He'd expected a detention at the most. "The police? But I wasn't doing anything."

"Breaking and entering," said Stringer smoothly. "That's what you were doing. That's what it's called."

"I didn't break in. I didn't go into the house, I told you. I didn't touch anything. The only place I went into was the gazebo, and it wasn't locked. And all I did was sit in there—" Luke stopped abruptly, disgusted by the fear in his voice, the rushing gabble of words.

"But your intention?" pursued Stringer. "How do I know what you might have been intending? I might have caught you just in time."

"I wouldn't do anything like that," protested Luke. "Break into a place. I wouldn't."

Deliberately, Stringer made no reply. He glanced down at the file, meaningfully, as if it had spoken out loud and called Luke a liar.

But Luke knew there was nothing of this kind in his record; nothing really serious, nothing to do with the police. It was just ordinary stuff, things like unpunctuality and being out of uniform, giving cheek, neglected work—the only really serious thing was what had happened on the station at Wood Hill with

Gosser. "Gross insubordination" was what they'd called it.

"At the very least, you've committed an act of trespass," said Stringer pompously. "And as I said, by rights I should inform the police."

Should. Luke grasped at the saving word. "Should" meant Stringer wasn't going to; he'd only been trying to scare him. He'd scared poor Mrs. Chambers, sneaking softly into the office where she sat at her desk leafing through the *Women's Weekly*. "File please!" he'd barked, and Mrs. Chambers had jumped up from her chair, frightened and flustered, as if she'd thought it might be her file the Deputy Principal wanted to see.

"Of course, for your parents' sake, I hesitate to bring in the police."

That was bullshit. As if Stringer cared about Mum and Dad. His mum would be scared of the Deputy Principal. His father might dislike the man but he'd be very careful with him because Stringer had the power to affect his son's place in the world. Dad would believe him, too. He'd believe anything Stringer chose to say.

It hadn't always been like that. Once Mum and Dad would have listened to Luke's side of the story and they'd even have taken his part. But Glendale was his third school; he'd been chucked out of Riversdale and St. Crispin's and last year he'd failed the HSC so badly it looked like he hadn't even tried.

"You'd be making it a whole lot easier for yourself if you told me exactly why you went into that house," said Stringer, "told me exactly what you thought you were doing in there."

Luke sat silent. How could he tell Stringer he'd gone to the gazebo because he'd wanted to remember the solid way he'd felt inside himself when he was a little kid? Stringer would think he was giving cheek, having him on. People like him always thought the really serious things were lies or jokes or "insubordination." Luke's eyes slid towards the window as he struggled to think of some explanation which might have a chance of going down. Out there on the green bank above the oval Mrs. Barlow was taking a class of Year 7 girls in calisthenics. The small girls rose slowly on their toes, skinny arms stretched wide; the girl on the end was wobbling.

Kids in Year 7 looked so little!

Stringer's voice ripped out, "*Will* you tell me what you were doing there?"

He'd have to tell him something. "It used to be my friend's house," he began uneasily. "I mean, I had this friend who lived there."

Stringer picked up his pen. "Name?" he demanded.

"What?"

"The name of this 'friend.' And even if the name checks out, Leman, I see no reason why you should be hanging round when, on your own admission, your 'friend' no longer lives there. No reason at all."

"Hamilton." Luke brought the name out with difficulty. "Alex Hamilton. But you won't be able to check, Mr. Stringer. They moved to America."

"When?" The pen was poised again.

"A long time back."

Stringer tapped the pen impatiently on his shiny desk. "How long, exactly?"

"Nineteen eighty-nine," muttered Luke, and he could feel the Deputy Principal's astonishment, like a charge of electricity zinging round the room.

"Are you trying to make a fool of me, Leman?"

"No, Mr. Stringer."

"Then let me get this straight. You went to that house, you skipped a class to do so, something a boy with your academic record can ill afford to do, you trespassed on private property, committed an *offense*—simply because, nine years ago, you had a friend who lived at that address?"

Luke nodded. He had the familiar feeling that something small and harmless was being twisted badly out of shape.

"Do you really expect me to believe that?"

"It's true."

"Very well." Stringer flung down his pen. "You refuse to give me any reasonable explanation for your actions—" He cleared his throat again. "—I must warn you now that expulsion is an option."

Expulsion. He couldn't mean it, could he? He was just trying to frighten him again. Or was he? Luke felt a stab of panic; if Stringer meant what he said this would be third time round. Third time round and less than a month before the final exams. He wouldn't even get a reference if he was expelled. Without a reference it would be hard to find a job—he'd end up on the scrapheap like Dad had always said.

"And expulsion would be unfortunate at this particular time," murmured Stringer. "Wouldn't it?"

"Yes, sir."

Footsteps sounded in the corridor outside, it was almost time for the bell. Stringer glanced at his watch; this boy had wasted enough of his time. He'd pass him on to Glenda Lewis, she might be able to get some sense out of him. Even get him working, if the boy knew the meaning of the word.

"Before any decision is made, I'd like you to see the school counselor." He swiveled round in his chair to consult the school timetable spread out across the wall. "Three o'clock tomorrow afternoon, I think. You have a study period then, and Mrs. Lewis happens to be free."

Mrs. Lewis was mostly free, thought Luke, because no one wanted to go to her, not if they could help it.

Stringer swung back to his desk; he took up his pen again and made a note in Luke's file. "Did you hear me, Leman? I want you to see Mrs. Lewis at 3 p.m. tomorrow."

"No," said Luke suddenly.

"What was that?"

"I said, 'No.' I don't want to see Mrs. Lewis."

Stringer stared at him. "And why is that?"

"She tells—" Luke stopped himself just in time; they hated it when you said something bad about another teacher. "I just don't want to see her," he mumbled.

Stringer's skinny lips grew thinner. "You have no choice in the matter, I'm afraid. I'm giving you a chance, Leman, and it may well be your last. Three o'clock tomorrow afternoon, sharp, or—" He let the rest hang.

The bell sounded. Doors banged, voices clamored, something heavy skidded along the passage outside, thudding into the wall. A boy's voice shouted, "I'll get you for that, Simmo, you just wait!"

Stringer pushed back his chair and strode to the door. He only had to open it and stand there and silence fell at once. A one-man peacekeeping force, thought Luke, though Stringer reminded him of war.

"That will be all for the present." Stringer turned back to Luke. "You may go."

Luke got to his feet. He'd meant to leave in silence, without another word, but halfway across the room something gave and the question came tumbling out of him in that voice he hated, the whining beggar's voice. "Will you be telling my parents? Will I be expelled?"

Stringer left him hanging still. He smiled at him coldly. "That will be up to you."

Treachery

"Just look at that!" Liz sprang up from the mountain of revision notes she was sharing with Caro and ran to the window. "Look at it!" she wailed, pressing her face to the glass, staring out at the dull grey afternoon, the sudden heavy shower of rain. "Can you believe it? Can you believe it's actually *October*?"

"Second month of spring."

"Spring!" scoffed Liz, tracing the passage of a fat raindrop running down the pane. "Oh, I just *hope* it's going to be fine for Saturday!" Her voice trembled, thinking of rain on Saturday, rain wrecking her barbecue, the very last party before the exams. Spoiling her *life*, she felt just then.

"It will be," Caro reassured her.

"In our dreams," sighed Liz. "And Caro, you *are* going to come, aren't you? You're not going to wait till the very last moment and then go and tell me it's too close to the exams and you've got all this work to do? You're not going to do that to me, are you?"

Caro laughed. "No," she said.

"Good!" Liz turned back to the window, watching the rain again. "You coming with Luke?" she asked softly, and though Caro couldn't see her friend's face she could tell from the tilt of her neat little head, a tautness in the way she held her neck and shoulders, exactly what expression Liz would be wearing—an expectant expression, like a magpie perched above a picnic table, waiting for crumbs.

Waiting for Caro to say something about Luke.

Caro never talked about Luke. He was so—complicated, so hard to explain, and Caro knew somehow that if she even started explaining, what she said would bring a stern look into Liz's eyes, a reproving edge to her voice.

And some things were private, anyway. Caro hated the way the girls clustered together at recess and lunchtime, talking on and on about their boyfriends. It was like a kind of striptease, she thought suddenly, as if they were all secretly chanting, "Get it off! Get it off! Get it off!" Nothing seemed to count except the sex. "What's he like?" they'd ask each other, and sex was what they really meant.

She'd been going out with Luke for months and they hadn't got past the kissing stage; that would seem weird for a start. And Luke wasn't even very good at kissing. He was nervous; his lips brushed hers lightly, then he'd hesitate, he'd draw back and look at her as if he was asking silently, "Is that all right?" Next time, Caro was always telling herself, next time she'd make it better; she'd hold him closer, kiss him slowly, properly; but then, when the time came, she never could. He made her as nervous as him.

"So are you coming with Luke?"

"Probably," replied Caro, trying to sound offhand.

Probably not, she thought. Luke didn't like Glendale parties. He wouldn't mix in. He stuck to her like glue and when she managed to get away she'd keep seeing him over her shoulder; no matter how crowded it was, her eyes would always find him, and he'd be standing on the edge of everything, gazing down into his glass, never saying more than a few words to anyone. A wave of irritation swept her suddenly; he never made an *effort*. Sometimes she wondered why she bothered.

It was the little things, she knew. Like the time they'd been having coffee in town, and this old Greek guy had brought them two special pastries he'd made himself. Caro hadn't been able to finish hers and when they were ready to leave Luke had whispered, "You'd better hide that cake in your handbag; he'll be hurt if you leave it."

Not one of the other guys she'd been out with would ever have thought of that, not in a million years. They wouldn't have noticed.

"Nick Lawson's going to be there."

"What?"

"Wake up, you're miles away. I said Nick Lawson's coming to my barbecue."

"So?" But Caro knew. She knew Liz thought she could do better for herself. They all did.

"He really fancies you."

"Fancies." Caro sneered at the word.

"Yeah, he does, Caro. What's wrong with that? And what's wrong with Nick Lawson? He's a nice guy."

"I didn't say he wasn't."

Liz tossed her head indignantly. "At least he's normal. Not like—" Her voice faltered for a moment and then she was brisk again, as if someone had to have some sense. "Look, Caro, I know you're going round with Luke, but that doesn't mean—"

Caro jumped up from the desk; notes and memos, summaries and summaries of summaries swirled round her like a snowstorm. Before she knew it she was halfway to the door.

"Where are you going?"

"Nowhere. Just to the bathroom for a minute."

Her face had gone hot, like it always did when Liz started putting on the pressure, hinting that Luke was a loser and Caro could do better for herself. Perhaps she even had a point, because some-times Caro felt Luke was driving her crazy. But all the same, it was her business.

And—Nick Lawson! Caro leaned over the basin and splashed cold water over her burning cheeks. Nick Lawson might be "a nice guy," but he was *boring*; all he ever talked about was foot-ball and workout programs, low-fat diets and—Caro straight-ened, tossing her head back, blinking the water from her eyes. So what was wrong with that? Was she getting to be a snob or something?

She grabbed a towel from the rail and buried her face in its thick soft folds; when she looked out again, surprising sunlight was scattered all over the bathroom walls. She stood on tiptoe, peering through the small high window out into the street; a narrow streak of blue had appeared above the horizon, a sword-slash in the sky. The street sparkled, light flashing from the leaves of trees and bushes, the puddles on the road.

And then she saw him, right down the end of the street, a small figure, a long way off, but she knew so well the funny way he walked, his shoulders hunched, his head lowered, eyes bent on the ground. Luke.

God, not *now*. Not when Liz was here. Liz would watch *him*, watch them both; study the way they stood together, whether they touched or not, how they looked and spoke to each other—and what all these things might mean. Liz was so *sharp*. And Luke would just—stand there. And when he'd gone, Liz would say, "I can't understand what you see in him, honestly."

Well, Caro wasn't having that.

But how could she stop him; how could she open the front door and tell him not to come in because Liz was here? How could she explain something like that?

She couldn't.

Caro stood there for a moment, frowning and biting at her lip, then she flung the towel away from her and ran from the bathroom, ran down the passage, skidding to a halt outside the kitchen door. "Mum," she said breathlessly, all in a rush, "Mum, Liz and I have just *got* to finish this work for tomorrow. If anyone comes, could you please say I'm out?"

Her mother was sliding a casserole into the oven. She had her back to Caro and she finished what she was doing before she answered, closing the oven door carefully and taking a long time wiping her hands on the dish towel.

"Mum—"

"I heard you." Her mother looked at her. "Anyone?" she asked slyly, and Caro knew she was really saying, "Even him?"

Caro flushed. Mum didn't like Luke. She'd heard all those stupid stories on the mothers' grapevine and believed the lot of them.

"Yes, anyone," said Caro. "Just say I'm out." Her voice was sharp, but the sharpness wasn't for Luke or even for her mother's little air of triumph; it was all for herself, her treachery to Luke.

But what else could she have done?

"You okay?" asked Liz as Caro came back into the room, closing the door behind her.

"Sure, why shouldn't I be?"

Liz shrugged. "No reason. I just thought you looked sort of—tense."

"Oh, it's just—all this." Caro waved at the mass of papers on the desk, the folders leaking from her schoolbag, the timetable glaring from the wall.

"Oh yes! Oh God, it's all so *horrible*!" cried Liz. "Do you know, when I wake up in the morning I actually feel sick, just thinking about the exams."

"It's only four more weeks," said Caro, sinking down on the bed. "Then it'll all be over."

"Don't *say* that! I'm never going to get everything done, there just isn't *time*!" Liz sat down on the bed next to Caro. "It's like being in a war, isn't it? Like sitting round waiting for the bombs to fall." Her voice rose to a wail. "And we haven't even got a shelter!"

Caro nodded, but she wasn't really paying much attention to Liz. She was listening for the sounds of Luke's arrival, praying Liz wouldn't hear anything. Her room was right at the back of the house; there was no way you could hear the bell from here, she told herself, or a knock, or voices at the door. But all the same she leapt up to switch on the radio and music like a great heart-beat swelled and thudded in the little room.

Full of Spikes

It was beautiful, thought Naomi, when she turned the page of the catalog and came upon the picture of the bright blue sweater. It was exactly right for Luke.

She laid the catalog down on the carpet and took the paper dolls out of their box. They weren't the kind you bought in toyshops; Cindy dolls and Barbie dolls who came with their clothes and shoes and wigs all ready so you couldn't find them things of their own or make up proper stories, because they looked all wrong. Naomi's dolls were ones she'd made herself; drawing their outlines on thick white cardboard, cutting slowly round the edges with her pink plastic kindergarten scissors. She'd wanted proper scissors, shiny silver ones, but Mum thought she was too little.

Her big sister, Molly, said Naomi's dolls all looked the same— like gingerbread men, she'd scoffed. But that was because Molly didn't look properly, so she hadn't noticed how their hair and faces were different; how the doll that was Luke had floppy brown hair and long eyelashes that were a darker brown, how the mother's hair went down to her shoulders in a smooth full curve, just like Mum's, and the father had big bushy eyebrows like Dad. "This one's you," Naomi had told Molly, holding up the doll with the tiny brown freckles on its nose, but her sister had just said, "Humph!" and stalked away.

Naomi arranged the dolls in a neat row on the carpet, then she took the catalog on her lap again, picked up the pink scissors, and cut carefully round the sleeve of the blue sweater, even more carefully round the collar, which was the hardest part, and then smoothly down the other sleeve and all the way round. The sweater came free and she held it up for a moment to look at the shine and the deep dark blue. Then she placed it beside the Luke doll and began to make up her story: how she was just back from Kinder, running up the path ahead of Mum, and there was Luke in the bright blue sweater waiting for them on the front verandah, home already even though it was only the middle of the afternoon. He ran down the steps and his face had the kind of shining, happy look which made you know he had something wonderful to tell.

"I've passed my exams!" he shouted. "I came top in Australia!" And then Dad was there, all pleased and smiling, and he *spoke* to Luke, he talked to him, just like he used to do. "We'll have a party!" he said.

"A picnic!" cried Mum.

Naomi reached out for the small box where she kept the dolls' food; she tipped it up and glossy roast chickens and glistening fish, a fat pig with an apple in its mouth, carrots and tomatoes and baked potatoes and bright green peas, cakes of all kinds— cream and chocolate and rainbow—all cut out of paper, tumbled down onto the floor.

But just then Mum came into the room. "Naomi," she began, and then stopped and said, "Oh!" bending down to untangle a long curl of paper which had twisted round the heel of her shoe. "Naomi," she began again, straightening up and crumpling the curl of paper in her hand, "I want you to tidy this stuff away, right now. Dinner will be ready in a few minutes."

Naomi cast a quick, worried glance towards the window. It was dark out there now; it was nearly night. "But Lukie isn't home," she said in a small voice.

"We can't wait any longer for Luke," replied her mother, and she strode to the window and pulled the curtains right across, making a harsh ripping sound.

"Where is he?" asked Naomi. "Where's Lukie?"

Her mother didn't answer. Naomi hated it when she wouldn't answer.

"Where is he?" she asked again.

Her mother turned from the window, but all she said was, "Hurry up now, Naomi, please. Get these things cleared away and take the boxes to your room. I can't understand why you don't play with them up there in the first place, instead of cluttering up the living room."

"I like it here," whispered Naomi, laying the dolls gently back in their box. She didn't like being up in her room when Lukie was late. The room got different then; it got smaller, and the furniture got larger and all sharp round the edges, as if the bed and the chair and the desk and chest of drawers were all waiting too, and asking themselves, over and over again, "Where's Lukie?"

When Naomi had put the boxes away she crept softly up the passage to her brother's room. She knew he wouldn't be there, but she felt she had to go in and look, all the same.

Lukie's room wasn't messy like Molly's, which had clothes and shoes and mugs and plates and magazines all over the floor. Mum had said she wasn't going to clean Molly's room any more and Molly had shouted, "Good! I don't want you to!" Lukie's room was tidy, like a room where no one lived. Everything was put away so it looked as if he didn't have anything except for the books and papers on the desk and the screwed-up pages in the wastebasket.

The air felt funny in here, like—like *spikes*. Naomi shivered. The door of the wardrobe was open a little and she tiptoed towards it to look inside at his clothes; right down the back she saw the blue blazer with the gold pocket Lukie had worn at his other school, the long blue trousers hanging down beneath it. She'd only been little when Luke had gone to that school. She reached out to touch the blazer and the hangers jangled faintly, like people with spooky voices talking softly to each other. Naomi's fingers flinched away. She closed the wardrobe door.

"Naomi!"

Mum was calling her. Naomi hurried from the room and then along the passage; halfway down the stairs she paused at the little round window on the landing and looked outside. It was proper night now. The dark street was empty and all along it the gates of the houses were closed, with everyone home and safe inside. She'd closed those gates herself, sneaking out of the house while Mum was upstairs, running quickly up one side of the street and then down the other, tugging and dragging them shut as she always did on those evenings when Lukie was late, because if all the gates weren't closed, if she left one single one of them open, even a little bit, the teeniest tiniest little bit, then something bad—

"Naomi!"

She ran on down the stairs.

They had tomato soup to start. "Where's Lukie?" Naomi asked again, but no one answered her.

As she took the first spoonful Naomi was sure, absolutely sure, that by the time she took the last one he'd be back, sitting in his place at the opposite side of the table where his plate and glass and knife and fork and spoon were all laid out. She listened for the sound of his feet on the path and the steps and the verandah, for the bang of the door and the thud of his schoolbag in the hall. She listened so hard her ears felt sore, but when the soup was finished Lukie still hadn't come home.

Her mother brought chicken casserole steaming in the big green dish; she spooned a wing and a slice of breast in red-brown gravy onto Naomi's plate. Everyone bent their heads and ate. No one mentioned Lukie. No one said he was late or asked each other where he might be even though it was night outside and he'd never been this late before. Naomi was scared to say his name again but when the clock in the hall chimed seven she just had to.

"Where's Lukie?"

Her mother frowned. Without looking up from her plate she said, "I wish you wouldn't keep on saying that, Naomi." But after a moment she put her fork down and said in a softer voice, "Luke has a lot of work to do, darling; he's probably down at the library."

Molly made a muffled snorting sound. "At the library!" she echoed, and rolled her eyes.

"That's enough, Molly." Mum's eyes jumped sideways towards Dad and then jumped back again.

Dad didn't like it if you talked about Lukie.

Dessert came. It was apple crumble and even a tiny spoonful felt dry and scratchy in Naomi's throat; she had to drink a whole glassful of milk before it would slide down, and her big swallows sounded so loud they seemed to fill the room. Someone touched her arm and when she looked round she saw Molly's big green eyes staring down at her. "Don't worry about Luke," Molly whispered. "He's okay. He's a big boy now, he can look after himself."

Naomi took up her spoon again and this time the apple crumble didn't stick so badly in her throat.

Then it began to rain. First big drops rattled and clattered on the tin roof of the verandah, like stones dropping from the sky, and a moment later the rain began to fall in earnest with a dull deep roar like a river rushing in a flood. Dad put down his spoon and rubbed his hands together briskly. "Brrr," he said, smiling round at them. "It's a night to be inside and no mistake."

Naomi jumped up and ran to the window. People came home when it rained. It was the time to be inside, like Dad had said. She could see the rain falling down through the streetlight, straight sharp lines of it, like an army of silver soldiers marching down the road. The lights in the houses opposite winked at her.

Naomi closed her eyes and put her lips against the windowpane. "Where's Lukie?" she whispered very, very softly, so none of them could hear her and get cross, and her warm breath made a misty circle on the glass.

Walking

After the session with Stringer, and a strange blurred hour which must have been double Biology, Luke found himself standing at the school gate. There was no sign of Caro, who sometimes waited for him there. No sign at all.

His feet just started walking.

He crisscrossed the suburb: down Jolimont Road and past the tennis courts, along Ferndale Avenue, round the corner and past the Primary School, then up Amhurst Drive and through the shopping center. Two Year 7 kids were hanging round outside the post office; as Luke went past they grinned and nudged each other. "Loopy Leman!" they giggled, but Luke didn't hear them, and he didn't notice when the rain started falling, or when the sun came out again.

Thoughts swam round in his head, slowly at first, then faster and faster, like a merry-go-round, a whirligig whose furious spinning hid the world from sight.

Was Stringer serious about expelling him?

If they did chuck him out, would he still be able to do his exams?

His parents—

Mrs. Lewis—

At the thought of Mrs. Lewis his step quickened. He didn't want to go to Mrs. Lewis; she told your secrets, she rang your parents up, she spread things round the school. Luke had heard all about her from Caro; Caro's friend Liz had gone to Mrs.

Lewis back in Year 8. Too young to know better, Liz said now. She'd thought she'd been pregnant and had been too scared to tell her parents. And Mrs. Lewis had been kind; she'd calmed Liz down and she hadn't rung her parents, she'd told her where to get a pregnancy test, and then Liz had found she wasn't pregnant after all.

She'd thought the whole business was over, but a week later she'd been standing with a group of kids outside the school canteen when Mrs. Lewis had walked past. Mrs. Lewis had called out to Liz, actually *called*, in a voice that everyone could hear, even the mums serving sausage rolls and donuts behind the counter—"Got your period yet, dear?"

And then there was Jennifer Brady, a girl in Year 10 who'd gone to Mrs. Lewis last year. A few weeks afterwards, word had somehow got round the school that Jennifer Brady was a schizophrenic. Not many kids at Glendale knew what the word really meant, but they'd started whispering how Jennifer heard the voices of angels and devils in her head, and how her parents were afraid each time she went into the bathroom and locked the door. Jennifer Brady had left Glendale suddenly, and no one knew what had happened to her.

Perhaps she'd just gone to another school, thought Luke hopefully, a good school like St. Catherine's where his sister Molly went. You could tell St. Catherine's was nice the moment you walked in the door; you could read it in the kids' faces, and the teachers' faces too, you could hear it in their voices, breathe it in the air. Yeah, that could be what had happened to Jennifer Brady, and St. Catherine's would have a good school counselor, too, one like Mr. Erlinger back at Riversdale. Luke's mate Danny Pearson had gone to Mr. Erlinger after his parents got divorced; he'd said Mr. Erlinger had helped him a lot.

Mrs. Lewis wasn't like Mr. Erlinger. Hardly anyone past Year 8 went to see her, unless they were desperate, or being forced, like Luke was being forced by Mr. Stringer. Because that had been the gist of Stringer's demand, he could see it now: go to the school counselor or get chucked out for sure. That was what Stringer had meant by "last chance." Going to Mrs. Lewis was his part of the bargain, but if he went, would Stringer keep his part?

Luke's feet stopped walking; he was in Birdwood Street, outside Caro's place.

Caro was his only friend at Glendale. Last year he'd managed to chum up with a kid called Artie Symons, but Artie had passed the HSC and got into his course and Luke had been left behind in a new Year 12. Two months back he'd started going out with Caro; he'd got to know her when they'd both been helping Ms. Brennan on the school magazine.

He swung the gate open and ran up to the porch, but as he raised his hand to the bell, he hesitated and his arm dropped to his side. It was past four and Caro would be working for sure; she was dead set on getting into Veterinary Science next year; she'd wanted to be a vet ever since she was a little girl. He shouldn't really interrupt her, not when she was working. He'd only stay a few minutes, he'd promised himself, just—he just wanted to talk to her for a bit.

He rang the bell. He knew it wasn't Caro coming down the hall; the footsteps were too heavy and the shape that loomed up behind the frosted glass was too short and bulky for slender Caro. It was Mrs. Hunter, Caro's mum.

Mrs. Hunter didn't open the screen but stood there behind it, staring out at him through the crisscrossed wire, her eyes fixing on the front of his sweater, on the big messy blotch where the ink had leaked from his Biro in Biology and run all over the place.

His hands were inky too.

"Oh, it's you, Luke," she said. "I suppose you're looking for Caroline."

Luke nodded, smiling at her, even though he didn't like Mrs. Hunter and he knew she wasn't happy about him going round with Caro.

She didn't return the smile. "Caroline's not here, I'm afraid. She's over at a friend's place; they're studying together. She won't be back till late."

"At Liz's?"

"I don't know, dear, I'm sure." Mrs. Hunter lifted a hand to her hair, tucking a strayed curl into place. "Caroline has so many friends, hasn't she? It's difficult to keep track."

Luke nodded again. He hitched up his schoolbag and Mrs. Hunter stared at that, too, narrowing her eyes, as if she could see right through the grubby canvas to the dog-eared blue folder inside, and somehow knew how he'd hardly even started on the assignment.

"I'll tell her you called." She flicked a switch beside the door and the porch lamp came on, flooding Luke with brilliant light. "Getting dark already," sighed Mrs. Hunter. "You'd better hurry home, dear." Her next sentence slithered at him like a snake. "You must have so much work to do."

As Luke closed the gate he saw a light on down the side of the house, in Caro's room. He turned his mind from the possibility that she might be in there and hurried away down the street, through the shopping center again, under the railway bridge, down Amhurst Drive towards the highway.

His house was very near now, less than half a block away, but he didn't want to go there just yet. This morning he'd promised himself he'd go straight home after school and put in a couple of hours' work before dinnertime. But now—now, he just didn't want to. No, it was worse than that; it was almost as if he couldn't, as if his feet simply wouldn't walk him there. The very thought of his room, his desk, of opening his schoolbag and taking out the blue folder—

He walked on up the hill towards the little park where Mum sometimes took Naomi to play. At its edge he passed an old lady with a dog who said, "Going to rain again," in a light happy voice like a child's, smiling at Luke as if she could see nothing wrong with him at all, as if he was just an ordinary kid coming home from school with ordinary thoughts inside his head.

He followed the narrow path through the trees towards the playground and sat down on a swing, drawing his long legs up beneath him. He liked the little park on the hill; it was a quiet peaceful place, so high above the suburb that in the daytime you could see for miles—miles and miles of rooftops and treetops with the towers and spires of the city shining in the distance. Now in the gathering dusk all this had become a great bowl of starry lights, and Luke sat swinging high above it, while the sharp spiky thoughts turned round and round in his head.

Could you really get expelled for sitting in a gazebo? Even if it belonged to strangers?

It seemed like such a small thing, but Luke knew there were people—and Stringer was one of them, for sure—who could take small things and turn them round, working a kind of magic, so the small things became huge and wrong and even criminal.

He'd been expelled from Riversdale for shaving off his hair. That had been small, and it had been a stupid thing to do; he could see that now, as he hadn't when he'd been fourteen. And the stupidest part was how he hadn't had a reason—he hadn't done it to set a fashion, to look tough or be different; he hadn't even done it as a protest. He'd just woken up one Monday morning and the sight of his Riversdale uniform laid out neatly on the chair—regulation shirt and blazer, trousers, tie, and socks and shoes, even regulation vest and underpants—had made him feel oddly breathless, as if all the air had gone out of the room.

Instead of opening the window, Luke had gone into the bathroom and shaved off all his hair.

They could have suspended him until it grew back—that's what Mum had said, even Dad had agreed. And Luke knew that if Mr. Erlinger hadn't been away on leave at the time he'd have fought to keep him at the school. But Mr. Erlinger *had* been away, and Riversdale had been the strictest kind of school. "Unreliable," the headmaster had written on his record and whenever Luke heard that word, even now, or saw it printed in a book or magazine, he had a kind of cringing feeling.

The reason he'd got the chuck from St. Crispin's hadn't been so small. On Wood Hill Station, in front of a whole mob of people, some of them kids and teachers from other private schools, Luke had bawled out Dr. Gosser, the senior science master; he'd told Gosser he was sick and twisted, he'd yelled at him: "You're the one who's giving the school a bad name!"

He'd had a reason for that, at least. St. Crispin's was near the station and Gosser had made it his business to patrol the platform at home-time, on the lookout for St. Crispin's boys who were "letting down the reputation of the school": smoking or swearing or horsing round. Or who looked, as Gosser put it, as if they might be thinking about it. He *named* boys, pointing his furled umbrella like a bone. "You, Jameson!" he'd bellow, "See me in my office first thing in the morning!" Everyone knew what that meant; within the privacy of St. Crispin's, Gosser used the cane.

The St. Crispin's boys were quiet on the platform, but once the train pulled out they ran wild; shrieking and shouting and hurtling down the aisles, pushing and jostling and punching and getting into fights, like demons freed from Hell.

On that particular afternoon, Luke's last one at St. Crispin's, two Year 10s who'd been named by Gosser back at the station had grabbed a little kid from Year 7 and thrust his arm through the closing doors. They'd held it there. "Gonna get your arm chopped off!" they'd jeered, and the little kid, his eyes bulging, sweat trickling down his cheeks like tears, had believed every word of it. When the doors bounced back and he was freed he'd sat down on the floor and sicked up on his shoes. He'd blubbered all the way to Carlingford and probably further down the line, but at Carlingford Luke had rushed from the train. He'd raced up the steps and over the footbridge and caught the next one back to Wood Hill where Gosser was still prowling the platform.

Because what had happened to that little kid had been Gosser's fault, just as surely as if he'd got hold of the little kid and stuck his arm through the door himself. That's how Luke saw it, anyway. Gosser scared people so much they couldn't wait to get their hands on someone smaller. And it made Luke mad, so mad he'd marched straight up to Gosser and told him he was evil …

He still felt he'd been right to do it. St. Crispin's hadn't thought so, of course, and neither had Luke's dad. "Think before you act!" he'd yelled. "You're ruining your bloody life!" "Feeling" you were right didn't matter, his dad had gone on; what mattered was what went on your record, because that was what people saw, and what they saw was Luke Leman expelled from a top school like St. Crispin's with "gross insubordination" written down beside his name. You couldn't get anywhere in the world on "feelings," Dad had warned him, you couldn't pass exams or make it into university and a profession. The only place you might get to was the scrapheap.

In the little park on the top of the hill, Luke swung slowly now, scuffing the toes of his sneakers in the damp woodchips underneath the swings. If Stringer expelled him he didn't know what his father would do. He wouldn't bawl him out, because ever since the mid-year exams Dad had stopped speaking to him. He *never* spoke to him, not even to say "hullo" or "pass the salt" at dinner. Dad acted like he wasn't there and it made Luke feel funny and insubstantial, as if perhaps he *wasn't* there. It made him walk in a different way when he was inside the house, treading lightly, as if he had no right to be there.

Perhaps he *wouldn't* be there soon; if Stringer chucked him out perhaps Dad would chuck him out as well. He might. Sometimes, at dinner or in the TV room, Luke would sense Dad looking at him; he could feel his eyes. Luke would keep his head down then, he wouldn't look up, he was afraid of what he might see.

It began to rain again. Luke jumped from the swing, grabbed his schoolbag, and set off through the park. It was late now, properly dark. Beyond the trees he could see the streetlights shining over in Hillcrest Avenue. God knows how long he'd been sitting there. The rain was getting heavier. He began to run.

Turning the corner into his own street, the idea that Stringer might have rung his home flashed into his mind—Mum and Dad might know already and they'd be waiting for him. As he came up the front path the door flew open and his heart leapt wildly, but it was only his little sister standing there.

"Lukie!" she called. "Lukie!"

He bounded up the steps and caught Naomi up in his arms, whirling her round and round. "How's my Queen of the Stars today?" he sang to her. "How are you, Queenie?"

Over her head he saw the hall was empty; Mum wasn't waiting for him there, with Dad standing silently behind her.

So Stringer hadn't rung.

Telephone

Luke's mother couldn't get to sleep.

Margaret had gone to bed before eleven and tossed and turned for half an hour. Sometimes she lay still and listened, alert for the sound of a door opening, footsteps in the passage, any indication Luke was still awake, and working.

He needed to work more than most. His marks in the mid-year exams had been so poor he could easily fail his HSC again. She couldn't understand it; he'd been such a bright little boy— what had gone wrong? Why— "Oh," sighed Margaret loudly, wishing Dan would wake and they could lie there and talk about their children like other parents did.

But such an ordinary little thing had somehow become impossible in their house. Dan wouldn't talk about Luke any more; he fobbed her off, all the time. And he wouldn't talk *to* Luke, not one word, not since those last exams. "He's on his own now," Dan had said. She couldn't see any point in such a punishment; it was cruel, it was—unnatural. The whole house felt strange; she often found herself walking on tiptoe.

Margaret flung the covers back. There was no point in lying here awake, going over and over the same old things; she'd go downstairs and make herself a cup of tea.

Tall and stately in her long blue dressing-gown, Margaret sailed softly through the house, but in the passage to the kitchen she caught her foot in something trap-like and stumbled against the wall. She peered down at the floor; an inch above it, the telephone cord stretched out like a trip-rope, snaking from the socket in the skirting board to the door of Molly's room. The door was closed.

Margaret studied the gap beneath; a tiny gleam of light showed in one corner, and darkness blocked the rest. That dark shape would be Molly, huddled down beside the stolen phone. In the quiet house Margaret could hear her daughter talking in a low sweet voice she never used for them.

"Oh!" Molly was saying. "Oh, I never said that!" She laughed, a sound of pure delight, like a careless sprinkle of small gold bells. "Oh, I did *not*!"

Margaret padded on towards the kitchen, telling herself it was wrong to eavesdrop on one's children.

Wasn't it?

But why were they so full of secrets? Why didn't they tell her things, like they'd done when they were smaller? Where did Luke go in the evenings, for instance, when he came home so late? Was he at the library, working? Was he studying at someone else's place? *Was* he working? What if he didn't pass this time? What was he going to *do*?

Margaret switched on the kitchen light and then stood blinking painfully in its glare; her head was seething, like a witch's cauldron on the boil. "That's *enough*," she told herself sternly. There was no point in worrying like this, working herself up; there was nothing to be done about Luke now.

Molly was another matter. Margaret seized the kettle from the stove and took it to the sink. Something could be done about Molly. She knew who Molly was talking to on the telephone, so late, past eleven on a weeknight, when there was school tomorrow.

Molly had a boyfriend.

Well, there was nothing wrong with that; her daughter was

sixteen, quite old enough to go out with boys. Molly had had a boyfriend when she was fourteen, a nice little lad called Brian Gibbon; they'd gone to films together and out to McDonald's for tea. Brian had come round to the house on Sunday afternoons and the pair of them had sat in the kitchen, eating cake and crisps and drinking Coke.

But this boyfriend was different.

Margaret had never seen him—and why hadn't she? Molly's mother asked herself, filling the kettle with water, crashing it back on the stove. Why was Molly hiding this one? She'd never spoken of him, not once. She'd never brought him home; when he came to pick her up in his car Molly waited outside in the street. And further up the street too, outside the Tibbetts' place where the big gum tree hid everything from view.

There could only be one reason for this secrecy, of course—there had to be something wrong with the boy, something Molly didn't want them to see. He could be a skinhead, covered with tattoos, or a wild-eyed New Age hippy with needle marks on his arms. He might not even be a boy, brooded Margaret, he could be a man, middle-aged, with a wife and children at home.

The kettle whistled, and Margaret's hand shook a little as she poured boiling water into her mug. She added a tea bag and sat down at the table.

She hadn't brought the matter up with Molly yet, because it was so awkward when you weren't sure of the facts, when you didn't even know the person's name. How could you start a conversation about someone you weren't supposed to know about?

And Molly was so aggressive these days, bristling all over, like a big fierce spider guarding the entrance to her lair. Margaret carried Molly's secret round in her heart all day, like a small cold pebble nudging against the heavier stone of Luke.

But tonight—yes, definitely—she was going to have it out with Molly. As soon as Molly put down the phone she was going to go in and suggest, firmly, that Molly invite her boyfriend home to meet the family. She would insist.

Margaret sipped her tea and let ten minutes pass. She carried her mug to the sink and rinsed it out; she rinsed it twice, slowly, dried it carefully, then took a deep breath, squared her shoulders and marched out into the hall.

Molly was still on the phone. Margaret went back to the kitchen and set the table for breakfast; she put out Weetbix and Cornflakes, honey and marmalade, bowls and plates and mugs and knives and forks and spoons. It took quite a long time, but when she'd finished Molly's sweet voice still murmured from behind her door. "I don't believe you!" she gurgled. "No, no! I don't!" Her tinkly laugh rang out again.

It was after eleven thirty and Margaret was tired, but she wouldn't give up, not now; she'd wait Molly out, however long it took. "Strike while the iron is hot," she told herself, and strode down the passage to the TV room, scooped Naomi's kindergarten smock from the back of the sofa, hunted out her workbox, and settled down to sew. She might as well get on with that torn hem while she was waiting.

Twenty minutes later, just as she was putting in the last few stitches, she heard Molly's door open, footsteps in the hallway, the jangle of the telephone banged down upon the table. Molly's footsteps receded, her door slammed. Crash! It shook the house, as if Molly thought no one but herself lived there. Margaret's lips tightened, she folded the smock and put her sewing box away and marched again into the hall.

There was no response when she knocked on her daughter's door. "Molly, it's me," she whispered. "Can I come in for a moment?"

A muffled grunt came through the door. Was that yes or no? But it was her house too, thought Margaret furiously. It was her home and her family, her life—wasn't it? She pushed the door open. Molly was lying in bed with all covers pulled up to her chin. "What do you want?" she demanded when she saw her mother. Her tone was rough, impatient; she sounded like a small storekeeper who'd shut up shop for the night.

"Just—" Margaret sat down on the edge of her daughter's bed. She sat lightly, as if she felt she had no right. "Just I'd like to talk to you about something, Molly."

"What?" Molly's eyes gleamed suspiciously from beneath her lashes.

Margaret picked a tiny thread of cotton from the quilt and rolled it round between her fingers.

"It's about—" she began hesitantly, and then stopped short, confused by the absence of the name she should have known.

"About what?" snapped Molly.

"What" indeed, thought Margaret, angry at Molly's tone. Her diffidence vanished suddenly. "Molly," she said, all in a rush, "darling, I'd very much like it if you'd bring your boyfriend home to tea on Sunday, and introduce him to us."

Then she held her breath. She expected Molly to bark, "What boyfriend?"—this was the way hostilities would begin.

But her daughter surprised her. Molly said nothing for a moment, and when she finally spoke her voice was quite soft, with just a tinge of scorn. "We're not getting married, you know," she said surprisingly.

Married? Margaret frowned, fresh alarm bells jangling in her head. Why should Molly say that? "Married?" she echoed fearfully.

Molly rose a little on her pillows. "Yes, married. Or engaged.

Bringing your boyfriend home to meet the family—that's what you do when you get engaged!" Leaning on one elbow, Molly surveyed her mother wearily. "Mum, girls don't bring their 'boyfriends' home to tea any more. Didn't you even know that?"

"They don't? But you used to bring Brian Gibbon home."

"Brian Gibbon!" Molly snorted. "Mum, that was when I was a kid. Brian Gibbon was kids' stuff."

So what was this? wondered Margaret.

Molly leaned forward, eyes flashing. "Why do you want Lionel to come to tea anyway?"

Lionel. So that was his name. It sounded dreadful to Margaret. Ominous. Old. The vision of the married man sharpened. "I told you, darling. Just so we can meet him, that's all."

Molly flung herself back on the pillows.

"Molly," Margaret began, but before she could get another word out, her daughter hissed, "I know why you want him to come here!"

"Why?"

Molly shot upright. Her face had a dark congested look, the sort of look that only shouting could relieve. "Because you don't trust me!" she yelled. "You don't trust me; you think I need watching all the time. You think I'm going to make a mess of everything, don't you? Ruin my life."

Margaret flushed. "No, no," she protested weakly. "It's not that, Molly—of course I don't think you're going to ruin your life." But she was lying through her teeth, and Molly knew it.

"Yes you do!" Molly's voice sank to a raw whisper. "You think I'm like *him*, don't you?"

"Him?" But even before Molly jerked her head towards the ceiling, her brother's room upstairs, Margaret knew who she meant.

"*Him*," said Molly again. "Luke. It's because of Luke, isn't it? You think I'm like him, you think I can't be trusted. You think I'm going to be the same kind of—" tears sprang suddenly into her eyes "—mess."

Mess. It was such a terrible word, thought Margaret, when you applied it to a human being.

Molly's tears came brimming over.

"Oh no, it's not like that," cried Margaret quickly. "It's got nothing to do with Luke. I don't think you're a bit like—" She stopped, horrified; what was she *saying*? She loved Luke, loved him best perhaps, yet here she was, sounding as if—Margaret glanced nervously towards the ceiling and then dropped her head, ashamed.

"Hopeless mess," Molly was sobbing, and whether the words referred to herself or Luke, Margaret didn't know. She put her arms round Molly, pressing her daughter's damp face into the stuff of the old blue dressing-gown. "Don't cry, darling," she pleaded, "please don't cry."

"I can cry if I want to," choked Molly, but as Margaret gently stroked her hair, the sobs grew quiet; Molly let herself be comforted and even settled back down to sleep. She lay still while her mother pulled the covers up and tucked her in. "Would you like the light out?" asked Margaret humbly, standing by the bed.

"Yes," replied Molly in a muffled voice.

Margaret reached for the switch but her hand froze midway and her eyes widened, arrested suddenly by the sight of her daughter's face.

What a fright Molly looked in the evenings! Her cheeks and forehead were plastered thickly with greasy skin cream, gobbets of it glistened like fat white maggots in her eyebrows. And her hair! It was plaited into many tiny rats' tails which stuck out stiffly from her head like darning needles from a cushion. So it would fizz out cloudily, splendidly, by day. So she'd look beautiful—for Lionel, thought Margaret sadly.

Molly's eyes slid open, sensing her mother's gaze. "What's the matter?" she demanded. "Why are you staring at me?"

"No reason, darling," said her mother, switching off the light.

Out in the passage, Margaret leaned against the wall for a moment, her shoulders slumped in defeat. She'd lost this round. She'd meant to find out about Lionel; what he did, whether he was still at school, or in a job, or unemployed. She'd meant to find out how old he was. She'd meant to ask—gently—why he collected Molly halfway up the street, instead of at her door. She'd found out nothing except his name. And somehow—how?—Molly had steered her away from insisting that he be brought home to tea. Tears, that was how. She'd been deflected from her purpose by Molly's tears, and that awful mention of Luke. Defeated.

It was always like this; she was no match for her children, she never had been, even when they were little. Years ago she'd gone to a course in Parent Effectiveness: the strategies she'd learned there hadn't worked at home. Luke had put his head on one side and gazed at her consideringly. "Mum, what's up with *you*?" he'd asked.

"She's training for the army," Molly had giggled. At ten, Molly had been a square stocky little girl, solid like Naomi. Luke, at twelve, was already becoming gangly. "Yeah," he'd agreed. "You know what? I think it's a revolution. A revolt!"

A sly glance had passed between them. "Mum's revolting!" they'd whooped at her, and rushed off laughing.

Back at Parent Effectiveness she'd listened to the other

mothers, faces glowing, reporting triumphs and successes. She'd wondered if they'd lied.

Margaret went upstairs.

Luke's room was right at the end of the passage, next to hers and Dan's. She knew it was late, well past midnight now, but he should be working; there were only four more weeks to go before the final exams. Monica Sleeton's daughter Amy was in Year 12 and she worked every night till one. All Amy's friends did, Monica had said. "It's a shame," she'd added, sighing. "They're so young, it shouldn't be like that." It shouldn't, either, Margaret thought. But it *was*, and that was that. If Luke was to have any chance at all—

She crept to his door and listened.

There was a dead silence inside. Her heart pounded, she hardly dared look downwards to the gap beneath the door. If a light showed there then at least he *could* be working, but if it was dark, that meant he'd given up tonight. Perhaps he always gave up. Perhaps he—

She looked down quickly—and her lips turned upwards in a sudden smile. The light was there!

"Luke," she called softly. "Are you busy, dear?"

"Yeah." His voice was gruff, impatient; she heard the faint rustle of paper, of pages being turned. He was working! He really was! "Would you like some Milo, or a cup of tea?"

"No thanks. I'm okay, Mum."

It was all right. He was working. It might turn out well after all, he might pass this time. Perhaps—you never knew—he might even pass well.

And as she walked the few steps down the passage, peace descended on Margaret for a moment, like a soft white dove folding its warm wings over her heart.

Arithmetic

Luke *had* been working.

If you could call it that. He'd sat at his desk, the few scattered notes for the Writing Folder spread before him, trying to think of an idea that went beyond a couple of lines, one line, a few words scrawled across a page. Scrawled, crossed out, put back again, doodles like bad dreams scribbled up and down the margins.

If you could call it working, that's what he'd been doing. He'd kept at it from eight o'clock till ten and then he'd crashed on his bed for a moment and sleep had overcome him, a thick dreamless sleep, sudden and violent, an axe falling from the sky.

He woke when his mother tapped on the door. "Luke, are you busy, dear?" He answered in the voice of an accomplished actor; the "yeah" sounded preoccupied, just a little irritable, as if she'd interrupted him in the middle of an idea. He even produced sound effects, leaning across the narrow space between the bed and desk to rustle at the sheets of paper, as if he might be riffling through his notes.

It worked; she went away.

He *hated* doing all this; lying, deceiving, pretending all the time. Deep down he felt he wasn't that kind of person.

He got out of bed and sat at the desk again, forcing his eyes to the sheet of paper he'd left lying there. At the top he'd written Stringer's phrase, "act of trespass," because it sounded like a good title for a poem, but he couldn't get beyond those words, they just sat there, and the prickly upright strokes of his handwriting were like a paling fence that shut him out.

There were six poems needed for the Writing Folder and he hadn't even written one. And it wasn't that he didn't want to work, like everybody thought. He *couldn't*, any more. Back in Primary School he'd been in the top reading group right from the very first grade; in Year 6 he'd won the English prize, and he'd been good at all his other subjects too. He'd done well at Riversdale, before he'd been chucked out.

It was at St. Crispin's that the thing had started happening, and it had begun with maths. He must have missed something, Luke thought now, some small, essential step along the way, without which nothing could make sense. He might have missed it because he hadn't been paying attention, like they'd said in his report. Dad had been furious when he'd seen the word "inattentive." He'd got out a piece of paper and done some maths himself; he'd divided the sum of Luke's school fees by the number of classes. Every lesson Luke wasted daydreaming, he'd told him, was fifty dollars down the drain.

Dad was in hock for Luke's private education—he'd wanted the best for his son and he'd taken out a bank loan; they hadn't been able to afford a holiday for years.

Right—so he'd started paying attention; he'd paid attention till his ears rang and his eyes burned, but the tangle of maths grew deeper; a jungle so thick and dark he couldn't see a thing.

Dad had found him a tutor (more money down the drain!) but it hadn't helped. The guy would explain a problem and then he'd ask, "Do you see?" And Luke would have to tell him that he didn't see, and then the guy would explain it all over again, slower, and still Luke couldn't understand. The tutor could have been talking in Dutch, or Swahili, because he couldn't understand it third time round, either. He'd stopped going to the tutor because he was embarrassed about seeming so thick, and it had been impossible to explain to Mum and Dad; they'd just thought he couldn't be stuffed to go.

You couldn't blame them, really, because that was what it looked like.

And the blindness, the locked-up feeling, had crossed over into Physics and Chemistry and then spread further, like a creeping sickness, into subjects you wouldn't think it would ever reach, subjects that had once been easy, like Biology and Geography and Legal Studies. In Year 10 at St. Crispin's the coordinator had told Mum and Dad he thought Luke might have trouble coping with Year 11. Luke had been there too, because St. Crispin's prided itself on including the students in such discussions, but the coordinator hadn't asked for his opinion, he'd only talked to Mum and Dad. And when he'd said that thing about "having trouble coping with Year 11," the *way* he'd said it, and the expression on his face—as if it wasn't a question of "might" but of absolute certainty—Luke had felt afraid.

You got the feeling you couldn't do it and the feeling became part of you, as if that was how you were. That was you. You were the kind of kid who couldn't cope, who would fail things.

Even English now. English had always been his best subject; he'd taken to it easily, like a person who doesn't have to learn to swim because the water is his home. But English for the HSC, exam English, was different; like a vast and shining ocean drained into a muddy puddle full of traps. You had to answer the questions in a certain way, you had to give the examiners the answers they were looking for; almost all the teachers said that. And then you started thinking how your answer, even if it felt right, might just be wrong.

Even a poem might be wrong.

Poetry had been his favorite thing, but now, when writing a few poems was just about the most important thing in his life, he couldn't seem to do it, his lines wilted like the little plants Mum brought home from the nursery sometimes; healthy and fresh at the start, shrivelling to nothing in the ground.

Passing English was so important it made you scared. Six poems for the Writing Folder. Six, by Monday, and it was Tuesday night. He glanced at his watch. No, it was Wednesday now.

Luke chewed at the end of his pen. The problem was how whenever he turned to any kind of schoolwork, he couldn't seem to *think*. His brain seized up, it seemed to shut, click! like a great stupid padlock snapping into place. And you couldn't explain a thing like that to anyone; it would just sound like an excuse, something he'd made up. That's what Mrs. Lewis would think, for sure. Or she'd think he was weird.

He snatched the Tertiary Entrance sheet from the back of the desk and skimmed quickly down the line of figures; the entrance scores for subjects like Law or Medicine were so high you'd have to get 901 in everything; it was like trying to touch the moon, for him.

Dad had wanted him to be a lawyer. Dad hadn't had much education himself. He'd left school at sixteen, and now he was forty-five and still in an office job at Bruxton Chemicals. He'd wanted better things for Luke, he'd wanted him to *be* somebody, to have a place in the world.

Well, Law was *out*. Luke crushed the score sheet in his fist and tossed it into the wastepaper basket; he'd be lucky to get into any kind of course. Numbers was what it was all about, he thought dismally. Arithmetic. Even if you wrote a poem as good as one of Shakespeare's, the kind of poem that could last a thousand years, you wouldn't pass Creative Writing 3B because you'd written one poem instead of six.

When he went to bed he couldn't get to sleep because the whirligig started, all those numbers spinning round in his head, and faces too, Dad's face turned away from him, Mum's face looking frightened, Stringer's black moustache jerking upwards on the word "expulsion."

Luke sat up. He slid on his knees across the bed and drew back the curtains from the window to look out at the night.

The houses of Orchard Court were all in darkness. Not a single light burned; there was no one sitting up late to read a book or write a letter or watch a movie; no one going out or coming home or just wandering into their garden to see what Orchard Court might look like at two o'clock in the morning in one of the very last years of the twentieth century.

Luke pulled the curtains across and lay down again, staring at the ceiling.

And then he heard the train. He heard it whistle, a long way off, and then louder, nearer; he heard the distant chatter of the wheels upon the rails. The train came every night at just this time—and it was puzzling, mysterious even, because everyone knew the last train from the city came through just after midnight. What was this train? It couldn't be a goods train headed for the country because the line didn't go anywhere; it ended just one station down.

Luke closed his eyes, and out there the train whistled again, further away now, faint and lonely sounding, one more time.

It was the night train, Luke decided sleepily, the train for night people, for all the ones who couldn't get to sleep, who lay awake and thought and thought, who had whirligigs inside their heads—and padlocks, great shiny padlocks, just like him.

Motherly

Mrs. Lewis's room was motherly, the sort of room you'd expect to find in a house rather than a school, with a table instead of a desk and two big friendly armchairs, a fluffy rug on the floor and pretty curtains at the window. A room you'd feel safe in.

And Mrs. Lewis looked motherly too, and safe; she was plump and middle-aged with a soft round face, pretty curly hair and a dimple showing in her cheek when she smiled. You could understand how a little kid would think she was nice, the sort of person you could tell things to, who really wanted to help.

But Luke wasn't a little kid; he didn't feel safe and he didn't want to tell her anything.

She kept on asking him about the gazebo, and he couldn't tell her why he'd gone there any more than he could have told Stringer. She'd think he was weird, for sure.

"What made you do such a thing? What was on your mind, Luke?"

"Nothing," he mumbled.

"Nothing?" echoed Mrs. Lewis. She smiled at him and the dimple deepened in her cheek, making Luke think of quicksand. "You had *nothing* on your mind? You mean, one minute you were in the playground, and the next you were in the backyard of a total stranger's place?"

He felt like yelling. He wanted to shout, "It wasn't a total stranger's place, not to me!" He didn't understand why they kept going on and on about his visit to the gazebo. It was only a little thing, and there were all these big things in his mind he didn't dare to tell. The gazebo didn't matter. "I thought—" he began, and then floundered into silence.

Mrs. Lewis edged closer. She was sitting right next to him, her chair drawn companionably near to his. "Yes?" she asked. The hem of her skirt brushed his knee and he moved sideways, putting a space between them.

"Nothing," he said again, clenching his jaw on the word, giving it an odd chewed sound.

"I can't help you if you won't help me, Luke."

"I know."

It was the wrong thing to say; she got angry at once. "At the very least, Luke, it was a silly thing to do. The sort of thing you could be expelled for."

Expelled. She said the word more loudly than the others, and Luke felt there was a little sound of gloating in it. In some aloof cool place within his mind, he knew Mrs. Lewis was the kind of person who should never have been a school counselor. She wanted to score off kids, he thought, she wanted to show she was right and you were wrong. It was bad luck for the kids at Glendale Secondary.

"Getting yourself into this silly mess! And when it's so close to the exams! But you haven't given a thought to that, have you, Luke? The exams."

He didn't answer. For months, he'd hardly thought of anything else.

"You're not doing very well in that department, are you? In your schoolwork, I mean."

"No."

"You don't seem to be making any effort. Getting your head down, getting stuck into it."

She had his file on her lap, the record, the person she thought was him. She tapped at its cover, sharply. "You don't seem to be trying at all."

"I do try," said Luke stiffly.

"It doesn't look like it."

He knew how it looked. Next Monday, if he was still at the school, Ms. Brennan would read his Writing Folder, six crappy poems he'd have written at the last minute, nothing like the ones he'd given her for the school magazine, and then even she would think he hadn't tried. That he couldn't be stuffed. And you couldn't blame her; how could she know he'd spent nights and nights, trying and trying—it hardly made sense to him.

"I do try," he repeated in a dull voice. He thought of the maths tutor, his patient voice repeating the problem, asking at the end of it, "Do you understand now?"

"Sometimes I can't seem to understand things," he began hesitantly. "I can't—"

Mrs. Lewis shook her head impatiently. "I can't believe that, Luke." She tapped at the file again. "You have a very high intelligence rating. You know that, don't you?"

He nodded. It was part of the problem, one of the reasons they thought he was lazy.

"That rating puts you in the top percentage of the population; it means you're absolutely capable—you should be sailing through. Shouldn't you?"

"I don't know."

"There's no question of you 'not being able to understand things.' That's nonsense, Luke. It's just an excuse, and a very bad one at that. There are plenty of children in this school who don't have your natural ability, who haven't had your advantages, and who manage perfectly. It's a question of *work*, Luke, of effort and organization and getting your head down. That's all. That's all there is to it."

There was a silence in the room. A little breath of air from outside the window puffed the curtains in and out; they made a sighing sound.

Luke said suddenly, "Am I really going to be expelled, Mrs. Lewis?"

She ignored the question. "Your parents, Luke—have you thought about them? They've given you every opportunity, they've made sacrifices for you—*two* private schools, Luke, all that money—and what have you done?" She slapped the file this time, punishing it. "Disappointed them, over and over again. You must be making them very unhappy. Don't you care about that?"

Of course he did. But if he told her the truth, how he hated the way he made them feel, she'd just say, "It doesn't look like it." He turned his head away but her voice came hunting after him. "Is there anything, anyone, you do care about, Luke?"

He thought of Naomi, saw her standing on the front porch, her face lit up to see him turning in the gate. The idea of even saying her name in this room made him feel sick.

"Luke, look at me!"

He turned his head slowly. Her eyes were dark with anger, her voice was shaking with it. "You're at a very crucial point in your life, Luke. The effort you put into your work these last few weeks—"

"Last few weeks." He felt a surge of hope; so they *were* going to keep him on. If they'd been going to chuck him out she wouldn't have used those words, would she?

"—will affect your whole life. You won't get another chance, Luke."

They always said this: the HSC was the big chance, the only

chance, and if you messed it up you could ruin your whole life. They said it so often and it became so familiar you accepted it as fact. But all at once Luke remembered something he'd read in the back of a Tertiary Studies handbook last summer. He hadn't really taken it in at the time because Dad had been so insistent about doing the HSC again, this year, but there were some universities where you could apply for admission when you were older, in your twenties. And they'd consider your application even if you hadn't done all that well back in school.

Mature Age Entry, that's what they'd called it. Perhaps there might be another chance then. "I was thinking—" he began.

"Yes?"

"I read about this thing called Mature Age Entry once, and I thought, well, maybe I could get into university later on. You know, work for a bit, and then—"

Mrs. Lewis shook her head.

He'd got it wrong somehow. Perhaps the handbook he'd been reading had been out of date.

"You mean I can't? You mean they don't have it any more?"

"Oh, they have it," said Mrs. Lewis. "They have it all right."

"So I could—"

She cut him short. "And children like you always think that's the answer. You think you'll put off all the study, all the work, for later."

"It's not—"

She brushed him aside again. "You may not have the opportunity when you're older, Luke. At twenty-five, you could have a family of your own to support. Have you thought of that?"

"No," replied Luke, startled.

"You could have a wife and children, you mightn't be able to *afford* to study. You wouldn't have the time or the money, all those things you take for granted now. But the main thing is—" She leaned towards him again, he could smell the make-up on her face, and it smelled like lollies, the kind little kids bought in tiny white paper bags. "—the main thing is, Luke, that you're not that kind of person."

"What?"

"The kind of person who's prepared to make an effort. You're not working *now*; what makes you think you'll settle down and make an effort when you're older? How do you know you won't just put it all off again?"

"I—"

"No, Luke. Procrastination—" and Luke could tell by the way she made her voice special that she was quoting something, "—procrastination is the thief of time."

There was nothing you could say to that. Luke stared down at his feet, surprised to see them looking so solid and ordinary, because he felt as if a great big piece had been knocked off him, and cracks spread everywhere.

The room was quiet again. The curtains billowed and sank back on the sill. Outside in the corridor someone in high heels walked briskly past.

"I don't know, I'm sure," said Mrs. Lewis wearily. "You children." She took her pen from the table and studied it carefully, clicking the point in and out. "Would you like to see someone?" she asked.

Luke froze. He knew she meant a psychologist, a shrink. He knew there were good ones, people like Mr. Erlinger at Riversdale. There might even be one he could talk to about the padlock feeling, who could maybe tell him what he could do to get rid of it. But he felt sure the psychologist Mrs. Lewis chose wouldn't be like that. He'd be like *her*, he'd be her kind of person.

He stole a quick sideways glance at her face. She thought there was something wrong with him, like she'd thought about Jennifer Brady.

The thing that really scared him now whenever he thought of Jennifer Brady was this: What if she hadn't been crazy, like everyone had said? What if she'd just answered the questions wrong? Or kept silent because she didn't want to talk about stuff that was private or might sound strange? What if she'd just been—a bit like him?

"I asked you if you wanted to see someone, Luke."

"No, I don't want to see anyone," he said violently. "I don't."

"That might not be a matter for you to decide." She rose from her chair and Luke rose too. She opened the door for him.

He still hadn't found out if they were going to expel him.

Mrs. Lewis stood at her door and watched the boy. He wandered vaguely down the corridor, heading in the wrong direction. Even the little Year 7 children, fresh to the school in February, knew there was no external door down there. He went right down to the end before he realized his mistake and then he just stood there, staring at the wall as if he couldn't understand why it was there.

Hopeless, sighed Mrs. Lewis. And so aggressive, too! The way he'd spoken to her! She locked her door and hurried round to Mr. Stringer's office, Luke's fat file beneath her arm. If she was quick she might just catch him before he left for home.

But Mr. Stringer had gone already. Mrs. Lewis went round to the staff room then; she felt like company, she really needed a chat after that little session. "I've just seen Luke Leman," she'd say, coming briskly through the door. "My goodness, that boy has some real problems!"

Some of the stuff in his file—good heavens! The way he'd shaved off his hair, taken the whole lot off one morning just before school. Completely out of the blue, and without a word of explanation. Neither rhyme nor reason. Irrational. And that incident on Wood Hill Station!

At least Phoebe had never done anything like that.

Phoebe was Mrs. Lewis's daughter. She was a problem Mrs. Lewis had never got round to solving. Sometimes Phoebe wouldn't speak to her mother, for no reason that Mrs. Lewis could see. She'd stay silent for days at a time, except for two words which she uttered, now and again, with a steely little smile, looking her mother up and down as if Mrs. Lewis was an article hanging in a shop, something that Phoebe herself would never buy.

That was a problem, yes. But it wasn't in the same class as the problems of Luke Leman, or some of these other children she saw.

The staff room was empty, so Mrs. Lewis went home. When she let herself in the front door Phoebe was standing right there in the hall, like a ghost beside the coat rack. She looked her mother up and down. "Silly bitch," she said, with her small cold steely smile.

Bafflement

For weeks, Luke had wanted to tell Caro about the padlock feeling. Twice he'd worked his courage up, even got the first few words out, but then he'd crumbled, clammed up. Changed the subject. He was afraid of losing her, he wasn't quite sure she'd understand, he could so easily picture her raising her solemn grey eyes to his face and saying, "Luke, I think it might be better if we didn't see each other for a while."

But today, he resolved, rounding the corner into her street, today he *would* tell her. He would.

"You're soaking wet," said Caro as he stood before her in the hall, rain dripping from the ends of his straggly hair and the sodden hem of his jacket.

"Just a bit."

Caro swept the drops from his shoulders and sleeves, and then stared in dismay at the muddy marks he'd left on Mum's new carpet.

"Caroline!"

"Quick!" At the sound of her mother's voice, Caro grabbed her coat from the hallstand. "Let's go." She hustled Luke towards the door.

"But it's raining!" protested her mother, coming out into the hall.

"It's stopped!" Caro was out on the porch already.

"But—"

"Back in a minute!" Caro slammed the door.

They trudged down Birdwood Street, through muddy puddles and drifts of wet-blown leaves, and Luke didn't say a word. Caro had known the moment she'd opened the door something was badly wrong; she'd seen it in his face. Had he guessed, yesterday, she'd been at home?

She'd wanted to ring him last night, but ringing Luke was just about impossible. It was one of the strange aspects of their relationship (something she'd hate Liz to find out), that she'd never once been to Luke's house; he'd never asked her. There was something wrong at home, she guessed; he never talked about his family. Ages back, she'd rung his house and a man had answered the phone—Luke's dad, she'd figured. But when she'd asked for Luke, the man had hung up on her.

Wrong number, Caro had thought, and tried again, but she'd got the same man and he'd put down the phone a second time. When she'd told Luke he'd said, "That's my dad, he's pretending I don't exist."

"How do you mean?" she'd asked, but Luke wouldn't say any more. Spooky.

So she never rang him up. And today she hadn't been able to find him at school; he hadn't been in the library for free-study period and he wasn't at the gate at home-time.

She glanced sideways at his face; he looked miserable, and she felt a sudden sharp little twinge of irritation; he was always so wrapped up in himself; if they broke up, he probably wouldn't even care.

As they turned the corner he spoke at last. "I went to see Mrs. Lewis today."

Caro stared at him, astounded. She could hardly believe her ears. "Why'd you do that? What did you talk to her about? She'll spread it all round, you know."

He shrugged. "Of course I know. But I didn't have any choice."

"How do you mean?"

"Stringer made me go."

Caro's hands clenched into fists deep in the pockets of her coat. He was in trouble again, you could bet. He was often in trouble and sometimes it was hard to see the reason why.

"What happened?"

She listened to the story of the gazebo, Stringer, and Mrs. Lewis, with a rising impatience. How did he get into these stupid messes? If he'd wanted to skip class why couldn't he hang out down the shopping center, like any other kid? Why did he have to go wandering into someone's yard? Why couldn't he do things normally?

"Why do you *do* this stuff?" she cried.

"It was nothing, Caro. I just wanted to see if the old place looked the same, that's all. How was I to know Stringer would come along?"

Caro kicked at a pile of sodden leaves. "He won't chuck you out, anyway. Not now."

"You think so?"

"He was just bullshitting you."

"That's what I thought but you can't be sure. He—"

Hates kids, finished Caro, though she didn't speak the words aloud. All Stringer cared about was "the school," whatever that was, if it wasn't them. She said wearily, "Oh Luke, you can't be sure of anything. It'll probably blow over. Lighten up a bit." She took his hand and squeezed it, to soften the sharpness in her words.

"Caro—"

"What?"

He drew a deep breath, as if he was going to tell her something important, something that made sense, for a change. And then he seemed to think better of it. "Oh nothing. Look!" He pointed to the house they were passing, where a clutch of bright balloons swung gaily from the gate. Through the window you could see a crowd of little kids rushing round the living room, shrieking and screaming, mouths stretched wide with joy.

"A party!"

She remembered Saturday. "Are you coming to Liz's barbecue?"

He shook his head. "Can't. I've got to get on with my Writing Folder. I haven't even started it."

"What!" Caro's heart lurched violently; she could have been the one who'd woken up this morning and found she hadn't done a thing. "You haven't even *started*?"

Straight away he took it back. "I've started, of course I have, but I've still got a lot to do. It's not easy, writing poetry."

"But you're good at it! You wrote those poems for the school magazine."

"That was different," he said quickly. "I wasn't writing them for an exam."

"But it's the same thing, Luke."

"No it isn't." They were standing at the intersection across from the shopping center, waiting for the lights to change. His voice was so loud that an old man beside them turned to stare.

"Look," blurted Luke, "I just can't—write stuff any more!" And before she could stop him, he lurched out blindly into the traffic, leaving her behind.

Cars hooted, someone shouted, Caro shut her eyes; she couldn't bear to look. When she opened them Luke was safely on the other side, and the old man was glaring at her, as if it was all her fault.

She caught up with Luke outside the record store; he was thumbing through the CDs on the sale table, tumbling them over, pretending to read the stuff on the back. "You could have been run over," she scolded, "rushing across like that."

"I knew I wouldn't," he said calmly.

Exasperated, Caro flung herself away from him. She stood on the edge of the pavement, next to the bus shelter, her back to him, gazing down the street. It was getting late now, some of the shops were closing. She'd have to go soon, Mum would be on the lookout, counting down the seconds. When Caro got in she'd rave about the mud on the carpet and then she'd tell her how much time she'd wasted wandering about with Luke, and how there were only four weeks to the exams. As if Caro didn't *know* that! How could you forget, with everyone reminding you all the time? The counting got you down. At least she was coping. Not like Luke. She couldn't understand why he always left everything till the last minute; it was always harder when you put things off, it made you panic. No wonder he was bunking off English.

It must be terrible to be like that, she thought. Terrible. Scary. She turned and went back to him, touching him gently on the shoulder. "You can do it," she said.

He swung round, startled. "What?"

"The Writing Folder. You can do it, Luke."

His face softened, he smiled at her. "Caro—"

"Yes?" she whispered.

He took that deep breath again. "See, what happens is, when I sit down to work, I—"

"What?" The word jumped from her mouth. It was too loud or something; he clammed up again.

"It doesn't matter." He spoke so sharply Caro felt she'd done something wrong. "C'mon." He seized her hand and pulled her on down the road towards the station, striding so fast she had to run to keep up. They passed the office with the big sign in the window: TOP MARK COACHING COLLEGE: RESULTS GUARANTEED. She saw his eyes flinch away from it.

A train hooted, sliding into the platform.

"Hey, you ever hear the night train?"

"What night train?"

"The one that goes by really late at night, round two o'clock."

"It couldn't be a train, Luke. There aren't any trains that late."

"It's a train," he insisted. "You can hear the whistle, and its wheels. You know that special clacking sound train wheels make?"

They were passing the barrier, commuters crowded through it, hurrying into the street, jostling each other, all alike in their neat grey suits. They looked like robots, thought Caro. "I hope we don't get like that," she said.

Luke didn't seem to hear her. He was staring past her shoulder, and his face looked shocked, as if he'd seen something frightening in the street. Caro turned, but all she saw was a postman on a motor scooter, his yellow raincoat gleaming, riding up the narrow lane towards the post office.

"Look, I've got to go," said Luke urgently.

"What?"

"Got to get home—I just thought of something. Will you be all right? To get home by yourself?"

"Of course I'll be all right," snapped Caro. "But why—" She couldn't believe it, he was going! Skipping away from her, backwards down the street, his eyes still on her face.

"It's Stringer!"

"*Stringer?*" Caro's eyes darted round, searching for the Deputy

Principal in the crowd. She couldn't see him. Why should he be there, anyway? She felt a kind of panic rising in her chest. What was going on? "*Luke!*"

He stood still. "He might have sent a letter to my folks!" he called across the heads of the startled commuters. "I just realized. I've got to check the mailbox. I've got to—"

"But—"

He turned and ran. He was gone. Just like that.

Caro walked away down the street, back towards home, and Mum. Her head was whirling, she didn't know what to think, it was all so—weird. She didn't know what was going on with him, what was happening, and she clenched her coat round her, suddenly feeling the cold, the icy dash of rain. She didn't even know if he really cared about her. How could he just run off and leave her like that? Her eyes stung, she felt an urge to cry; a misery, a bafflement, invaded her.

It was always like this.

How could they go on?

Shutting the Gates

Margaret was sorting the washing from the drier; shirts and skirts and socks and underwear, jeans and towels and table-cloths. And after this, she thought, there might be time to wash Naomi's hair before dinner. There'd only be the four of them tonight because Dan was working late. He often worked late these days and sometimes she thought he did it to avoid the sight of Luke. And to avoid *her*, because he knew she wanted to talk to him about the way he was treating Luke, this awful, stupid, childish silence that only made things worse.

Dan was hard to pin down. This morning when she woke he was already in the bathroom, and when she tried to talk, he'd snapped at her, "Not now, can't you see I'm shaving?" It was impossible to talk at breakfast because the children were there, and in the evenings he went to bed early and seemed to fall asleep the moment his head touched the pillow. He'd gone out of range, she thought, like a lone blip vanishing from a radar screen.

Margaret paused in her folding, pushing the damp sticky hair back from her face. It was hot in the laundry, airless; the whole house was airless. It was past six o'clock and Luke wasn't home either. She worried when he didn't come straight home from school; she found herself waiting, listening for his footsteps just like Naomi did. It was useless asking him where he'd been: he'd give her an answer, but how could she be sure that answer was the truth? He—

The door burst open. Because she'd been thinking of Luke,

Margaret expected to see him standing there. But it was only her daughter.

"Have you got my big white T-shirt?" Molly demanded. "I need it for gym tomorrow."

"It's over there on the table."

Molly squeezed past her mother and set about the stack of folded laundry. She pulled things out and tossed them aside, but Margaret said nothing, waiting for the long explosive hiss she knew would come.

"Oh!" Molly held the T-shirt out in front of her.

Margaret kept her head down, swiftly she hid the bright red socks beneath a towel.

"It's pink!" wailed Molly.

"Oh dear."

"Why do you *do* that?" shouted Molly. "Why do you always make my white things pink? Why can't you be more careful? Don't you know you're supposed to wash white things separately?"

"Of course I know."

"Then why do you keep on doing it? Why do you always wreck my things?"

"I've told you before, Molly. I'm in a rush, I get home from work, I've a thousand things to do, I don't have time to check what's in the basket. I just don't notice."

"You never notice anything!" cried Molly. "You never do things properly!"

"Now listen," began Margaret, but Molly interrupted in a cold stern voice. "You're not a proper mother."

Margaret didn't ask her what she meant by that. "Then do it yourself!" she snapped. "Do your own washing in future!"

"All right, I will!" Clutching the spoiled T-shirt to her breast,

Molly stormed out of the laundry, slamming the door behind her.

Margaret took the red socks from underneath the towel and tossed them onto the table. She folded another pair of jeans and two of Dan's shirts. She straightened the pile that Molly had mussed about. Her hands moved slowly, methodically, but she felt like grabbing the clothes and tearing them apart, ripping them into pieces and throwing them about, sitting down in the mess and having a good noisy cry.

Why did they speak to her like that? As if she was nothing more than a servant? What right did they have? Why did they go on and on, the pair of them, Molly and Luke, about her washing and her cooking, and things they left lying round the house and expected her to find?

And then her hands stilled. It was only Molly who raged at her now, she realized. Luke didn't do it any more; he never went on about his clothes and what she'd cooked for dinner; he hadn't done it for a long, long time. Last week she'd accidentally dyed his new white socks a sickly greenish shade, and he hadn't said a word. Suddenly, she wished he'd roared. She wished he'd come up to her, holding the socks in his hands, yelling like he used to do, "Mum, what's this? What do you think you're *doing*?"

He'd gone quiet.

Margaret left the laundry and walked down the passage to the living room. Now it was time to wash Naomi's hair.

But her younger daughter wasn't in the room. Her boxes and cutouts, her paper dolls and catalogs lay scattered on the floor, but there was no sign of Naomi. She wasn't in the kitchen or the bathroom and she wasn't in her room upstairs. The little bed was empty, and the chair beside the desk; from the top of the chest of drawers the row of china cats stared back at Margaret, with knowing smiles between their painted whiskers. Luke had given her those.

"Naomi!" she called, rushing down the hallway, pushing open doors and peering into rooms, beginning to feel afraid. She ran downstairs to Molly's room.

Molly was lying on her bed gazing dreamily at a photograph cupped secretly inside her hand. The T-shirt, forgotten, lay crumpled in a heap on the carpet.

"Molly," said Margaret breathlessly. "Have you seen Naomi?"

"Naomi?" Molly looked up blankly.

"Yes, Naomi. Your little sister."

Molly slid the photograph beneath her pillow. "She was in the living room," she offered vaguely, "with all that junk of hers."

"Well, she isn't there now. She's not in the house! She's gone!"

"Gone?" Molly leaned on one elbow and surveyed her mother calmly. "Where would she go?"

"I don't know!"

"Oh, relax, Mum, for God's sake. Of course she hasn't gone—she's round the house somewhere; you just haven't looked properly."

As if Naomi was a missing pair of sunglasses, thought Margaret furiously as she flew back down the hall, through the kitchen, out the back door. "Naomi!" she called across the dark backyard. "Naomi! Naomi!"

Naomi had gone to shut the gates. She'd waited till her mother was busy in the laundry and then crept out through the back door, closing it softly behind her. At the front gate she stood still for a moment, looking up and down the street, the way she did every evening when Luke was late: first, to see if he was coming, and then to make sure there was no one else about.

It was almost dark, but not quite, because you could still see the colors in the sky; a band of pink on the horizon, the pearly grey of the clouds and the deep blue spaces in between. A funny old moon was rising, like a person with a lumpy bumpy face climbing over the rooftops to spy on her. "Go away!" hissed Naomi, crouching down low, making herself small, running along the footpath to the house next door.

The gate was closed there, so she hurried on to the next house, where the Tibbetts lived; Mr. and Mrs. Tibbett and Sammy Tibbett, who was hardly more than a baby and didn't even go to Kinder yet. Their gate was closed too; it was almost always shut so Sammy couldn't run out into the street.

Next door the gate was open just a little bit and Naomi shut it quickly, she hardly even had to stop, but the next gate was wide open and she had to creep inside to reach hold of it properly. That was all right because the curtains in the front windows were closed and there was no one there to see her.

Now Naomi had reached the end of their street. It was a small street, a court, with just four houses on each side and their own house down at the bottom. She crossed the road, looking carefully to the left and then to the right and then to the left again, even though not many cars came into their street. When a car did come, Naomi would squeeze down small against the fences, hiding in their shadows, still and very quiet. Once Mr. Tibbett had come driving down the road and seen her; he'd stopped his car and asked her what she was doing, out by herself so late. Naomi hadn't known what to say at first, and then she'd made up a lie; she'd said she was looking for her tennis ball.

Mr. Tibbett had got out of his car and helped her search along the nature strips and in the bushes and Naomi had felt sorry about all the trouble he was taking, but she couldn't tell him that.

Mr. Tibbett had said she shouldn't ever come out in the dark by herself, even if she'd lost something. "Wait till the morning," he'd told her.

The first house on this side of the street had no gate, only a driveway. Driveways didn't count and Naomi hurried on to the next house. The gate squeaked here, but it was only a small squeak, like a very tiny mouse. And now Naomi's footsteps slowed and she began to creep, because the next house belonged to Mrs. Jackson. Two high wooden gates enclosed her driveway; when Mr. Jackson was home the gates were closed, but when he was out they were left standing open, pushed right back against the fence.

Two days ago Mrs. Jackson had caught her; she'd come down the verandah steps and across the lawn so fast that Naomi hadn't even heard her. "Just what do you think you're doing, Naomi Leman?" she'd demanded in a sharp, cross voice and when Naomi hadn't told her, Mrs. Jackson had become even crosser. "Don't let me catch you again!" she'd said.

Naomi prayed the gates would be closed tonight, but no, they were standing open, ready for Mr. Jackson's car. She glanced towards the house; there was a light on above the verandah and the living-room windows were lit as well, the curtains drawn right back; Naomi could see Mrs. Jackson inside, sitting in a big armchair, turning the pages of a magazine.

She tiptoed towards the gates, holding her breath, her eyes fixed on the windows. Mrs. Jackson's head was bent right over the magazine now, she'd stopped turning the pages and was reading something. Naomi darted into the driveway and seized the edge of the first gate; it was big and heavy and wedged firmly on the concrete of the drive.

Naomi tugged and tugged.

Bang! A door slammed. Mrs. Jackson had come out onto the

verandah. Naomi slid behind the gate, squeezing herself into the narrow space against the fence. She couldn't see Mrs. Jackson from there, but she knew Mrs. Jackson couldn't have seen her, or she'd have started yelling. She'd come out to see if Mr. Jackson's car was coming. Naomi held her breath and listened, waiting for the door to slam again; she waited so long her legs began to ache and she felt like crying.

How could she close the gates with Mrs. Jackson up there on the verandah? And what if Mr. Jackson came home?

She had to close the gates. She had to. Each night she had to close all the gates along the street, otherwise—otherwise something would happen to Lukie.

Naomi knew this, she knew it in her skin and bones and blood and hair: if she didn't close all the gates in Orchard Court something bad would happen to Lukie.

Bang! The verandah door slammed shut again. Naomi peeped out from behind the gate. Mrs. Jackson was back inside the living room; she had the big armchair turned round now, with its back towards the window; she was watching television. Naomi came out from her hiding place and grasped the gate with both hands, lifting it clear of the concrete—and now it moved quickly, suddenly, sliding from her hands and rushing to the edge of the drive with a long scraping sound that made Naomi freeze.

But it was all right; Mrs. Jackson hadn't heard, she stayed in her armchair with her eyes fixed on the television. Carefully, holding fast to the side, Naomi closed the second gate. Just as the latch clicked shut she heard her mother calling her. "Naomi! Naomi!"

Naomi ran past the last house, which had no fence or gates at all, only a lawn that came right up to the footpath. She slipped in through her own gate and hurried down the side path. When she came round the corner of the house there was her mother standing at the back door.

"Naomi, where have you been?"

"Nowhere."

"Nowhere?"

"I was just round the side," lied Naomi, "I was—looking for my tennis ball."

"But I've been calling you for ages. Why didn't you answer?"

Naomi looked down. From the corner of her eye she saw the wooden lattice which fenced in the stumps of the house; there was no lattice round the side, you could crawl in underneath. "It—it went under the house," she told her mother. "The ball. I was under there."

She did look as if she might have been under the house; her clothes were dusty from the narrow space behind Mrs. Jackson's gate, and there was a cobweb in her hair.

Margaret brushed the cobweb away. "Look at the state of you!" she scolded. "And haven't I told you repeatedly not to go under the house? You could get bitten by a spider or something. And Naomi, when you hear me call you, I want you to come straight away. Do you hear me?"

Naomi nodded. "Yes, Mum," she said.

Night Wolves

Down at the station, the moment he'd seen that postman, Luke had felt strangely certain Stringer had sent a letter to his parents to say he'd been expelled. Stringer was just the type who'd do the thing by mail, so he wouldn't have to look at their faces or listen to their shocked and pleading voices.

A letter bomb. Stringer *was* a bit like a terrorist; he had that same blank look about his eyes, as if he didn't understand people were real.

But there was no letter. The box was empty and there were only bills lying on the table in the hall. And Mum and Dad said nothing. But Luke still couldn't stop worrying. He couldn't figure out if Stringer really did mean to expel him or if he was only bullshitting, like Caro said. Luke couldn't be sure, either way; and not knowing was almost as bad as having the thing happen; the uncertainty made you feel like you were walking through tricky undergrowth, holding your breath so tight your chest hurt, waiting for a trap to spring.

It was hopeless trying to work. "You can do it," Caro had said, but he'd been sitting in his room since dinner and he hadn't done a thing. The very sight of that dog-eared blue folder gave him a faint, queasy feeling, as if he'd eaten something bad.

Tomorrow was Thursday. What if, on Sunday night, he was still sitting here and he still couldn't think of anything? What if that happened? What if it did? Could it? It was crazy, this padlock feeling in his head. He wished he'd been able to tell Caro about it this afternoon. He'd *almost* told her, but then he'd drawn back like he always did.

There was no one else he could tell, really. He didn't want to tell Ms. Brennan because she'd be disappointed in him; and Mum would just get upset. As for Dad—well, you couldn't talk to someone who wouldn't talk to you, who pretended you weren't even there.

When his dad had first gone silent, Luke had thought the punishment would only last a few days and he'd just have to hold his breath and tread softly till things got back to normal.

But it had gone on and on. He'd tried to break the silence; he'd find little pieces in the newspaper, odd spots and funny paragraphs that he and Dad would once have laughed about together. He'd go to the TV room where his father was sitting and say, "Hey, Dad, listen to this!" and read the paragraph out loud. Halfway through, or even sooner, he'd realize Dad wasn't going to say anything; then Luke's voice would go all funny, but he'd keep on reading the paragraph right to the very end because somehow it seemed even worse to stop.

Silence.

He used to wait for a moment then, hanging in the doorway, still hoping, because he could never quite believe his dad would keep on doing this to him.

Then he'd walk away, treading lightly, and actually *feeling* lighter, as if something inside him had melted away.

He didn't bother with Dad anymore.

Alex Hamilton was the person he could have explained things to. Alex wouldn't have thought the padlock thing was weird, he'd have found it interesting, and he'd have wanted to talk about it for ages, discussing every little detail. He'd have understood how it could happen to someone and that person might really be all right, not stupid or weird or crazy or anything. But Alex was gone; it was useless even to think of him.

He should have told Caro.

Caro! Suddenly he saw her, standing in the street outside the station, pulling her coat around her as if she was cold, staring at him with a baffled expression in her eyes.

He'd left her there! He'd rushed off, the moment he saw the postman and thought of Stringer's letter, leaving her to walk home by herself.

Luke jumped up and ran downstairs to the phone. He dialed Caro's number. The phone rang for a long time over in her house, and then Mr. Hunter's voice answered, thick and dazed with sleep. "Yes? Who's this? Who is it?" and before Luke could get in an answer, Mr. Hunter barked, "Do you know what bloody time it is?"

The time. Luke glanced down at his watch and the figures sprang out at him: 1:35. He hadn't known it was so late; he'd thought it was only about eleven.

"Are you the boyfriend?" Mr. Hunter demanded. "What the hell do you think you're doing ringing up at this time of night?"

The phone dropped from Luke's nerveless hand. He'd messed that up all right. He hadn't said a word, yet somehow Mr. Hunter had guessed at once it was him. How?

Luke trailed slowly up the stairs. Tomorrow he'd have to explain the call to Caro. "Why do you *do* these things?" she'd say.

As he tiptoed down the passage he heard a faint cry from Naomi's room. He pushed the door open and found his little sister sitting up in bed, crouched in the corner against the wall. He sat down beside her. "Hey, what's the matter, Queen of the Stars? What's up?"

Naomi gulped. "There's wolves in here."

Luke rolled his eyes in the way that always made her smile. "Watch me," he whispered, putting a finger to his lips. He got up from the bed and crept over to the wardrobe, flinging wide the doors.

"Ooh!" squealed Naomi, shrinking back against the wall, but Luke shook his head. "No wolves in there." He crouched down on the carpet and peered right under the bed. "Or there." He crossed to the chest of drawers and slid the top drawer out, grabbed a long striped sock and waved it in the air.

Naomi giggled.

"Seen any wolves?" he asked the row of china cats, bending down close to listen for their answers. "They haven't seen a thing," he told his sister.

Naomi pointed to the ceiling. "Up there," she said.

Luke raised his eyes. Light from the streetlamp outside the window quivered and danced on the ceiling. He could see why she'd thought of wolves; the dancing shadows had a lean grey stealthy look.

"That's just the shadows of the trees outside," he explained. "It's leaves blowing in the wind, that's all." He sat down on the bed again.

"Night wolves," said Naomi. "I thought it was night wolves come to get me."

"They'd never dare," said Luke. "They wouldn't be game. Anyway, there aren't any wolves in Australia, Queenie."

"Thought wolves," whispered Naomi.

"What?" Luke leaned closer; he couldn't have heard her properly.

"They're thought wolves, the night wolves," she said.

A chill stole down Luke's spine. But she couldn't mean what

it sounded like, he told himself; how late at night the scary thoughts came out from their corners and prowled your mind like wolves. She couldn't mean that; Naomi wasn't that kind of kid. She was a strong little kid. She meant "made-up" wolves, that was all.

"What's the matter, Lukie?"

"Nothing." He picked up her hand; it felt warm and solid in his own. "Night wolves, thought wolves, black wolves, brown wolves, big wolves, little wolves, any old wolves—they'd never get you, they'd be too scared. They'd never come near the Queen of the Stars."

"Never?"

"Never ever."

He let her hand drop and got up from the bed. He went round to the window and drew the curtains close. "See," he said, pointing to the ceiling. "All gone."

Naomi nodded and lay down again. Luke pulled up the eiderdown, settling it round her. "Okay?" he asked.

"Okay," she said.

His mother was outside in the passage.

"Luke, what are you doing? Have you been disturbing Naomi?"

"She was awake," said Luke. "She had a bad dream."

His mother put her hand on the door.

"She's all right now," he said quickly. "She's gone back to sleep."

"Oh," said his mother.

He watched her face. Hope and doubt battled plainly in her eyes. She thought he might be lying, but she also thought he might be telling the truth. She still believed in him a bit, he knew. She hadn't written him off, like Dad.

Hope won out: his mother smiled at him. "Sorry," she said softly.

It was two o'clock. Far away, the night train whistled, sliding round the curve behind the golf course, speeding on towards the station. He could almost see it; the dark wheels chattering on the shiny rails, the line of lighted windows, the blank faces of the night people staring straight ahead.

"Hear that?" he asked his mother.

"What?"

"That train. The night train."

"I can't hear anything." She frowned. "There aren't any trains this time of night. Luke, will you go to bed, *please*. It's after two o'clock."

"Okay."

"Good night," she said more gently.

"Good night."

Seven Thirty in the Morning

Right, now for it! Margaret raised her chin, stood tall, and knocked on Molly's door.

"What do you want?" growled Molly. Never, "Good morning, Mum," or even, "Come in," thought Margaret. They had to make you feel unwelcome all the time.

Molly was sitting on her bed, combing her rats' tails out. One side of her hair was soft and cloudy, the other still bound up, and the little plaits had been so tightly braided they'd pulled her eye askew. It gave her face a strange lopsided look; one half soft and young, the other foxy and old and sharp. Mismatched, thought Margaret, like a puzzle in *Cole's Funny Picture Book*.

She got to the point at once. "I want no nonsense, Molly," she said firmly. "I want you to bring that boy to tea on Sunday so we can meet him. *This* Sunday," she added.

Molly said nothing. She turned her face from her mother and stared straight at the wall, as if she liked it better. Being difficult.

But really, Molly just wanted to hide. She hated this idea of Mum's; she didn't want to hear about it. To tea on Sunday! To tea, in *this* house! Molly's throat quivered, and a procession of awful pictures flitted through her mind.

Lionel coming in through the front door and all of them standing ready, waiting to look him over, as if he was a mail-order bride. Mum being mumsy, acting like Molly and Lionel were engaged or something; Dad giving him the third degree:

What was he studying? What were his plans for a career? What did his father do? Dad wouldn't bother to ask what Lionel's mum did, of course; he was too old-fashioned for that.

Naomi would stare at poor Lionel and then go rushing off to make one of her stupid paper dolls; it would have round pudgy limbs and currant eyes and no clothes on; she'd come and lay it on Lionel's knee. "That's you," she'd say.

Worst of all was Luke. He'd be at home, you could bet on it. He was mostly out, wandering round the suburb like a dero, but that day he'd stay in, for sure. She could picture the scene exactly; he'd come shuffling down the stairs and though it was Sunday, he'd be wearing his filthy old school uniform because he never seemed to change his clothes these days. His long greasy hair would be sticking out all over the place, making him look like a mad professor who had something nasty growing in the cellar.

He'd call her "Captain Coolibah," the dopey name he'd had for her when she'd been a little kid. "Captain Coolibah's got quite a temper," he'd say to Lionel. "You're a brave man, Gunga Din."

Even if he didn't say anything, she didn't want Lionel getting a look at the kind of loser she had for a brother—this loser Luke had gone and turned himself into, for no reason, for no bloody *reason*! Every now and then, out at a party or club, some kid she didn't even know would sidle up to Molly and ask, "Are you Luke Leman's sister?" Molly hated that.

She didn't want Lionel to come to this house, ever. Their house wasn't normal; it was horrible, it was a madhouse.

Sometimes the place was really, really quiet, so quiet even the floorboards seemed afraid to creak. It made your chest feel tight; it made you want to yell and scream to crack that silence right across. But sometimes it cracked all by itself. It could burst, at any moment. You'd be sitting in your room and you'd hear whispers, and the whispers would rise like the wind that brings a storm and then suddenly people would be rushing round and shouting and crying—all over nothing, over any little thing. It was like a whirligig. Oh, she hated this house—as soon as she finished school she was moving out, for sure.

She wasn't bringing Lionel here, no she wasn't! Mum couldn't make her, and Dad couldn't either. Dad didn't know about Lionel; Dad never really noticed anything unless it had to do with Luke. Luke was all he ever cared about, even though he never talked to him. Mum wouldn't have told Dad about Lionel because Dad had gone so quiet he was scary. Mum was frightened of Dad and Dad was frightened about Luke and even Naomi was frightened now—that spooky way she had of asking "Where's Lukie?" every time Luke was late home for dinner.

It was all Luke's fault. Why had he got like this? Why did he keep on messing up at school when he was really clever? Why had he turned himself into this loser when there was no reason, when once he'd been so different? He'd been her favorite person in the world. A terrible sadness squeezed at Molly's heart; she almost forgot the problem of Lionel coming to tea, even though Mum was standing there, waiting for an answer. Molly flung herself down on the pillows and burst into tears.

Margaret rushed over. "Molly, what's the matter?"

Molly kept on crying, clutching at her stomach.

"Are you sick?"

"No," gasped Molly.

"Is something wrong at school?"

"No."

"Is it—is it something to do with Lionel?"

God, Mum was an idiot. Molly rolled her head from side to

side, her hands still clawing at her stomach.

Margaret's eyes riveted on those desperate hands, an ancient suspicion tugged at the ends of her nerves. "You're not pregnant, are you, Molly?"

Molly sat up at once. Her tears stopped instantly. "No, I'm not *pregnant*." Her voice was cold, it was icy. She gazed at her mother with contempt. Mum was out of the Ark, like Dad. They were Mr. and Mrs. Noah! "Do you know what's wrong with you, Mum?" she demanded.

"What?"

"You always think the worst. The worst of *us*. You think like a newspaper, a really *old* newspaper, from the 1950s or something, all sexist and ageist and full of crap. You think there's something wrong with us and we're going to end up in a mess just because we're not as old as you. If it's a boy, you think he'll get on drugs and end up on the scrapheap—" Molly's voice rose to a shriek. "What's *that*? What's a scrapheap, Mum?"

"I don't know," gasped Margaret. It wasn't her word anyway. It was Dan's, the one he used for Luke. "Molly, I—"

Molly wasn't listening. She stormed on. "And if it's a girl you think she'll get boy mad and sleep round and get pregnant. You think, just because we're kids, we're stupid! Well, I'm not! You're the one who's stupid! You and Dad! It's stupid to think like that!"

Margaret sprang up from the bed, her hand up to her cheek as if she'd just been slapped. But she wasn't giving in this time. Oh, no. "Sunday afternoon," she repeated firmly. "Remember that, Molly. *This* Sunday."

Fifteen minutes later, clawing through the laundry basket— where were her gym shorts?—Molly sensed a shadow darkening the room. She looked up and saw her brother lounging in the doorway. *Looking* at her; taking in her swollen face and puffy red-rimmed eyes. "What are you staring at?" she snarled.

Luke wagged his head. "Why do you do it, Captain Coolibah?" He grinned at her slyly, rolling his eyes.

"Don't call me that!"

"You used to like it."

"That was when I was little." Molly snatched her gym shorts from underneath a tablecloth. They were filthy! She rounded on her brother. "Why do I do *what*?"

"You know—" he jerked his head towards the kitchen, where breakfast was going on. "Stir Mum up. Get her going."

"What about *you*?" shrieked Molly, pushing past him through the door. "What about *you*?"

That shut him up. But only for a moment. He came charging after her down the passage. "What *about* me?" he shouted.

Molly didn't answer; she rushed into the downstairs bathroom, slamming the door behind her.

Luke pounded on it with his fists. "What *about* me?" he roared. "What *about* me?"

Their father was reading the paper when the row broke out. Their mother was spreading marmalade onto a piece of toast. Naomi was carefully pouring milk onto her Rice Bubbles. She bent her head low over her bowl, the jug still in her hand, but there was so much banging and shouting she couldn't hear the snap! crackle! pop!

Naomi looked up at her mother. "They're fighting," she said. "Molly's fighting with Luke, in the—" She broke off with a little gasp. The milk had poured right over the rim of her bowl and down into her lap.

"Oh," cried Margaret. "Oh, Naomi! Look what you've done! Just look!" She jumped up to look for the dishcloth, while outside in the passage the shouting and hammering went on and on.

Dan Leman put down his paper. He pushed his chair back and strode out into the passage. "Molly!" he called, even though Luke was making most of the noise. He didn't look at Luke; his gaze swerved round him, like an elegant lady skirting a beggar in a busy shopping street. He looked at the picture on the wall instead: a big white sailing ship breasting stormy waves.

"It's seven thirty in the morning," Dan Leman told the sailing ship. "It's seven thirty in the morning and let's have some peace and quiet!"

Quiet came then; everyone shut up. But as for peace, thought Margaret, mopping the milk from Naomi's soaking lap, peace might never come again.

An Affective Problem

She was so spiteful! thought Rosa Brennan, watching Mrs. Lewis edging up to Stringer in the staff room, her cheeks flushed, eyes bright, telling on Luke Leman.

Because that's what it was, really: telling, like a little girl sticking up her hand in class to tell the teacher someone in the back was being naughty.

"I couldn't get anything out of him," Mrs. Lewis was complaining. "He simply refused to talk."

"Sullen and uncooperative," agreed Stringer, and Bob Grace, off to his Year 10 Physics class, paused in the doorway to catch Rosa's eye, and shook his head sympathetically.

Rosa felt a twinge of irritation. It was fine being sympathetic, but why didn't Bob *say* something? Why didn't they all say something, stand up to Stringer and Mrs. Lewis? There was hardly a teacher on the staff who didn't dislike Stringer's methods and Mrs. Lewis's gossip.

"He didn't seem to follow what I said, half the time," Mrs. Lewis went on happily. "It's quite difficult to believe he has such a high intelligence rating."

Stringer considered this for a moment. "The figure could contain some sort of error," he said. "The tests were done elsewhere."

"And he only passed two subjects last year, didn't he? That's not the sort of result you'd expect from a clever child."

"Well, he's lazy, obviously."

It was too much for Rosa. "Look, I know his marks don't show it," she burst out, "but I honestly believe Luke Leman is one of the most gifted students I've ever had."

"Really?" Mrs. Lewis widened her eyes.

"Yes, really."

"But he's doing so badly; if he was as intelligent as he's supposed to be—"

"He could simply be anxious. Anxiety can do that to you, paralyze your mind, make it difficult to work properly. Haven't you ever felt so worried about something that you can't concentrate, can't think straight?"

"No," said Mrs. Lewis flatly.

"And clever children can do badly at school," Rosa went on. "Seventy-five per cent of the high-school dropouts in America have above average IQs."

Stringer raised his eyebrows. That was all, but the tiny gesture made Rosa feel suddenly uncertain. She knew she'd come across that U.S. dropout figure somewhere, but she couldn't remember the exact place. Had she read it in an educational journal? A book? Heard it on the radio, perhaps? If Stringer asked her for the source, she wouldn't be able to name it; he'd think she'd made it up. And had she got the figure right? It had been surprisingly high, but had it been as much as seventy-five per cent? Might it have been only fifty? And—

Rosa checked herself. She was letting him get to her. That was how Stringer operated, keeping silent, making you feel weak and uncertain, sure to be wrong somehow. She said quietly, "You can see Luke has a good mind from his conversation."

"Conversation!" scoffed Mrs. Lewis.

"And there's his poetry, too."

"Schizophrenics often have a talent for poetry, don't they?"

asked Mrs. Lewis softly.

Rosa flushed angrily. "Luke doesn't have that problem, Mrs. Lewis. And you shouldn't start these rumors."

Mrs. Lewis glared at her. "The boy has an affective problem," she said darkly.

"An affective problem?"

"He has no affect," repeated Mrs. Lewis. She was talking to Stringer now, as if she'd given up on Rosa. "No ability to care about the feelings of others, to—relate. He has hardly any friends, haven't you noticed?" She paused for a moment and then her voice rose harshly. "That young man doesn't care about anything or anyone!"

Stringer nodded, but Rosa said violently, "Of course he cares! He's an isolated boy with very little confidence, that's all. He came here from another school—"

"Two schools," corrected Stringer, with a tiny smile. He raised a finger and wagged it at Rosa. "*Two* schools, Ms. Brennan."

"All right, two schools," said Rosa crossly. "It doesn't make any difference how many; it's difficult to make friends in a Year 12 where all the other students have been together since Year 7."

"Difficult for him," said Mrs. Lewis. "And this relationship with Caroline Hunter, have you heard about that?"

"Yes."

"Are they an item, do you think?"

"I couldn't say," replied Rosa coldly.

"Because I think that would be a great pity. Caroline Hunter is a nice girl, and doing very well. I was thinking of having a word with her, I'm sure her parents—"

"Please don't do that!" Rosa cried. "Please don't interfere, Mrs. Lewis. Luke has hardly anyone to talk to as it is, and he's under so much pressure—"

"*All* the Year 12 children are under pressure, Ms. Brennan," said Mrs. Lewis crisply. "But they learn how to cope. They don't go round hiding in gazebos."

Stringer interrupted, clearing his throat with a small commanding bark. "Yes, this gazebo matter: I've given it considerable thought and as it's so close to the exams, I've decided against any action."

"Action?" queried Rosa. "What kind of action?"

"Well, in normal circumstances it could be a matter for expulsion. Suspension, certainly."

"Expulsion!" Rosa gazed at him, dumbfounded. "You can't be serious! Expelling a Year 12 student for walking through someone's backyard. It's ridiculous!"

Ridiculous. The word seemed to quiver in the air. Mrs. Lewis flashed Rosa a swift reproving look.

Stringer blinked. His face went still and cold and dangerous as ice, and Rosa realized suddenly that this little pompous man frightened her.

"As I said," Stringer repeated, "I will *not* be taking any action. It's the parents one has to consider in this sort of case. The Lemans are decent people, and they've given the boy every advantage it was possible to give. They have my heartfelt pity."

His words had an unexpected effect on Mrs. Lewis. Her pretty features wavered, as if she'd slipped down underwater, her blue eyes took on a cloudy, absent expression; she might have been listening to stray feet wandering on her grave. "These children!" she wailed. "They just throw things away! You give them everything, you give and give and give and give—and they just throw it all back in your face!"

Rosa stood still, transfixed; in that moment she felt deeply sorry for Mrs. Lewis. All this talk of parents and ungrateful children had reminded the school counselor of her own ungrateful child. She was railing about poor Phoebe, and in her voice there was something like grief.

Anyone could see.

But Stringer didn't. He stared at Mrs. Lewis with a faint surprised distaste. He blinked again. "Er, yes," he said.

There was something blind about him, thought Rosa. He was like some small sightless animal thrown up from a dark burrow by a great disturbance in the earth, his head bobbing and batting at the air, dazzled by the light.

She picked up her bag and pushed past the pair of them, heading for the door.

In the Park

It was past six o'clock, and all over the suburb Year 12 kids were settling down to work, or thinking about doing it; turning pages and scribbling notes and pressing keys, listening all the time for the welcome lovely sound of their mums' voices calling them to dinner.

They "looked different," their aunties and uncles kept telling them; shocking, their grannies said: some of them had grown fat, eating biscuits and chocolate while they studied; some had gone thin because they couldn't be bothered to eat. There wasn't time to eat, the thin kids told their mums, and everything tasted like cardboard anyway, like paper, like textbooks and revision notes and copies of old examination papers. Everything tasted like doubt.

Liz's chin had come out in a crop of pimples, big ones, as big as ripe strawberries, Liz thought, peering into the mirror. She knew she'd brought them on by worrying about rain spoiling her barbecue on Saturday. "Mostly fine," the long-range weather forecast promised, but that could mean anything.

"You're mad to have a party so close to the exams," her mum kept saying, but Liz replied that she'd go mad if she didn't. "We'd all go mad," she'd told her mum. "We *need* that party."

Caro hadn't been at school; she'd caught a cold and lay in bed with a sore throat and her nose blocked up and an ache behind her eyes. She couldn't study because of the ache and it panicked her, losing a whole day. When she fell asleep she dreamed of

Luke. "I don't think we should see each other for a while," he told her, and she woke in her crumpled sweaty sheets with a feeling of surprise, because she was the one who should have said that.

Molly lay on her bed too, and daydreamed about Lionel; she pictured the way his hair grew from his forehead in a sweet springing wave, the dear shape of his nose, his lips—and then quite suddenly she thought of her brother, the way he used to be. Molly rolled over on the bed and hid her face in the pillow.

In her kitchen Rosa Brennan was preparing dinner. She was making gnocchi: little balls of mashed potato, herbs, and semolina. She tipped them into a big pot of steaming soup; they sank to the bottom and in a little while swam back up to the surface, wreathed in tiny bubbles like goldfish waiting to be fed. "Ah," breathed Rosa, and her little dog Penn raised his head expectantly, nose quivering.

"Not now, Penn," Rosa told him, taking his lead from the hook on the wall. "First we'll go for a walk."

It was a clear cold night and the stars shone down from an icy sky. There'd be a frost tomorrow, you could feel it in the air. At the edge of the park Rosa unclipped the lead and the little dog bounded away across the grass, running in widening circles, but Rosa stayed where she was, leaning against a tree.

These days she felt tired after school, weary as a person twice her age. And tonight she couldn't seem to stop thinking about that scene in the staff room this afternoon, and how when she'd been young she and her friends had giggled about teachers like Stringer and Mrs. Lewis. Troglodytes, they'd called them. She'd *laughed*. Now they scared her, haunting the edges of her dreams. They were like dangerous children, she thought, the kind of children who said "please" and "thank you" nicely and then went down the back to pull the wings off flies.

"Chin up, Rosa," she imagined her old dad saying. "Don't let things get you down. What use would you be then?" And he was right, too.

Over near the playground Penn began to bark excitedly; he'd got something trapped, bailed up, a cat or maybe even a possum. But as she hurried towards the playground Rosa saw there was someone sitting on the swings. Not a child, but the big huddled shape of a man. She felt a twinge of fear; the park was deserted and it was a long way back to the lighted houses of Hillcrest Avenue.

"Penn!" she called, but the little dog kept right on barking, bouncing stiff-legged on the grass. The man got up from the swing and she saw he was only a boy; as he passed under the lamp at the edge of the playground she recognized Luke Leman; his distinctive way of walking, shoulders hunched, head lowered as if he was looking for something in the grass. What was he doing here, so late, sitting on the children's swings?

"Luke!" she called, and at once the little dog flung himself upon him, barking joyously, scrabbling at the boy's trousers with his muddy paws.

"Down!" ordered Rosa. "Get down, Penn!"

Penn took no notice. Rosa caught him by the collar and fastened on the lead. "I'm sorry," she apologized to Luke. "He's covered you with mud."

"That's all right." Luke swatted half-heartedly at his shabby Glendale trousers. "They're old anyway." He bent down to pat Penn's head.

"Are you on your way home?" asked Rosa. "Would you like to walk with me? I'm just down in Hillcrest Avenue; that's on your way, isn't it?"

The boy nodded, but she could sense his reluctance and she knew he was afraid she was going to chatter on about school, prattle away about exams and study and assignments, even ask how he was getting on with his Writing Folder. He walked beside her because she'd asked him and he'd been too polite to refuse, but it was like walking with a balloon that bobbed and tugged at its string, longing to get away into the sky.

They came out from the park and into the street. In the lighted windows of the houses evening scenes were playing; families were making dinner, sitting round tables, watching the news on TV. A little girl fed her cat in a kitchen and a tiny boy in a highchair suddenly upturned his bowl on his head and started crying as his dinner trickled down his cheeks. His dad picked up an empty bowl from the table and did the same; the little boy stopped crying and began to laugh.

"Look at that!" Rosa turned to Luke, smiling, but the boy's face had gathered strangely, as if he was about to cry.

"My dad won't talk to me," he blurted. "He hasn't talked to me for months. When he sees me, when I pass him in the hall or somewhere, he walks right past me like I'm not even there—as if I don't exist."

Rosa was appalled. "Oh, Luke, I'm sorry."

"He doesn't care what happens to me any more. He's written me off."

"I'm sure he hasn't. I'm sure he does care about you, really." Rosa's reply sounded false and hurried; she wasn't sure at all. Parents could get spooky sometimes.

"No," said Luke, his voice quite plain and matter-of-fact. "He doesn't care about me; he just worries about me, that's all."

"He wouldn't worry if he didn't care." She knew what he meant though; she saw it all the time at Parent-Teacher nights:

the worry and fret and fear. And Year 12 was like a vortex, she thought, sucking everybody in. A black hole. She could understand how kids found it hard to believe there was light on the other side.

"It's like a bad joke," Luke muttered.

"What is?"

"Everything." He flashed her a sudden sidelong grin. "Me."

"You're not a bad joke, Luke. You should never think that way about yourself. Never."

He didn't answer, but his face softened, making him look younger. About thirteen, she thought, and felt a stab of hatred for the silent Mr. Leman. She wanted to say, "Look, don't worry so much about the exams; even if you fail them it's not the end of the world."

But she couldn't. Because if she did he might just stop working and these last few weeks could be crucial to his marks. To his getting out of there.

They'd reached her gate. Penn bounded away from them up the path towards the door. "This is my place," said Rosa.

"Oh." He ducked his head awkwardly. "I'll be off then."

"Just a minute. Look, Luke, things will change for you, I promise. I know it's difficult now, at school, but it won't always be like that. When you leave, when you start at university—"

His face closed like a fist.

Oh God, she'd spoiled it. She shouldn't have mentioned university, she shouldn't have said that word. It meant exams, it meant everything. It had slipped out before she thought. Force of habit.

"Luke!" she called, but he was already running, he was halfway down the hill.

She *should* have told him not to worry, that it wasn't the end of the world if he failed. She should have. As Rosa turned into her gate she felt a chilling sense of something missed, slipped sadly from her hand. Let go.

Coming Home

Dan Leman was on his way home from work. He drove mechanically, stopping at the red lights, cruising through the green, scarcely aware of the traffic around him or the suburbs flashing by. Some evenings, turning into his own street, the familiar houses caught him by surprise; he'd have not the slightest recollection of the journey between Bruxton Chemicals and his home.

Luke would have been on his mind.

The boy had been on his mind tonight because Margaret had rung again, caught him in the office; she'd accused him of being unfair to Luke! She'd got to him somehow, because the moment he'd started the car he'd begun to wonder if he might be mistaken in believing Luke would fail the HSC again. His midyear report had been shabby, a disgrace when you considered that he was doing the same work he'd tackled last year, but he *had* scraped through, except for maths, and it was possible, just possible, he might pass this time, collect enough marks to get into something, somewhere.

An Arts degree perhaps, at some small place—and with an Arts degree he might be able to get into the Public Service, and once he was there, in a proper job, he might pull his socks up at last and try to make something of himself. Grow up. It wasn't the same as being a doctor or a lawyer, but beggars can't be choosers and you could get somewhere in the Public Service, if you worked, if you—

Dan Leman's hands, big and bony like his son's, suddenly tightened on the driving wheel. He was doing it again! He was starting to hope, giving way to something that might be hardly more than daydream. Luke would turn it into daydream. You had to face facts with a boy like Luke, you had to expect the worst and prepare for it, so you wouldn't be disappointed all over again, made into a fool. Yes, Luke would probably fail, and he'd go on the dole, end up on the scrapheap, because that was the kind of thing Luke did. That was Luke and he had to accept it.

He hated what the boy had brought upon them; not just the disappointment and bafflement, or the anger that rose at the sight of the kid throwing away his chances, chucking every advantage they'd struggled to give him straight back in their faces—but the shame.

The shame that colored his face when Bob Teale at the office, relating the triumphs of his son and daughter—the daughter at Med School, the son on some high-powered exchange to the States—would ask him: "And how's Luke doing?"

The shame of having to sit in school offices, cap in hand, pleading for another chance. Last time, down at Glendale Secondary, Margaret's eyes had been shiny with tears.

Luke had made them into beggars, that's what he'd done.

He hated coming home in the evenings, he couldn't bear to see the boy; the way he sat at the dinner table, his head bowed over his plate, his hands clumsy with the knife and fork. Or in the TV room, slouched on the sofa, averting his face when Dan came into the room, flinching away as if he expected to be hit. He'd never struck Luke in his life; he didn't believe in hitting children. He still didn't believe in it; that wasn't what had gone wrong.

"Please talk to Luke," Margaret had pleaded, but what good

would talking to him do? Margaret had accused him of being cruel, but she'd got it wrong; she didn't understand that he avoided Luke to save *himself*, to keep his distance; getting up close was the way he'd been hurt before. Talking to the boy would only start the hopes up all over again.

He wished he didn't have to actually *see* him. Because sometimes, looking at Luke, a terrible pity would wrench at him and he couldn't stop himself thinking that somehow, somewhere, it might just be their fault. His fault.

How the hell did he get that idea? Hadn't they done everything for the boy? The private schools, the extra lessons, the tutors: they'd tried everything. How could it be their fault?

Yet the idea lurked inside him like a secret sickness no one had found out. What could he—Dan's hands gripped the steering wheel again. Stop it! he ordered himself. Stop thinking about him!

He glanced through the window and saw that he was in his own suburb, almost home, halfway up Chelmsford Road, near the library.

The library. When Luke came home late, when he didn't show up till just on dinner, Margaret would always say he was probably down at the library, working. No one believed her, unless Naomi did. Margaret didn't believe it herself.

But suddenly, halfway up Chelmsford Road, Dan began to wonder if they might be wrong. What if all this time Luke really had been down in the library, heading down there after school, putting in a few hours' work in peace and quiet before he came back home? Keeping mum about it because he didn't want to disappoint them all over again?

Dan parked the car.

He walked into the library.

Luke wasn't there, of course.

Of *course*.

But seated in one of the carrels, notes and books spread out before him, was a boy about Luke's age in the dark-blue blazer of St. Crispin's.

Dan stared at the boy. He took in everything: the orderly arrangement of the books and papers on the desk, the way the boy's hand held the pen, elegantly, easily, while notes flowed out upon the page, the confident expression on his face.

He hated that boy. He hated him because he wasn't Luke.

And yet he loved him too. He was everything—everything—he'd wanted Luke to be. That Luke could have been, if he'd tried.

Dan left the library and went back to his car. He took the long way home, circling past the golf course and the bowling green, up into the richer streets beyond. He drove along Firbank Crescent, past the tall houses in their deep secluded gardens, the houses where doctors and lawyers lived, and people who had a place in the world.

The Letter

When Luke got home from the park he found Stringer's letter waiting in the mailbox.

He hadn't expected it. He'd started feeling safer that day. All through morning classes, every time the PA system had begun to crackle with a message, he'd tensed up, thinking it might be for him, the call to the office to tell him he'd been expelled. When there'd been no summons by lunchtime he'd started to relax, and by the time school was over he'd decided Caro had been right: Stringer had been bullshitting.

He'd gone round to Caro's place but no one had answered the door, then he'd gone to the park because it was a place he still found peaceful, and when you felt peaceful the idea of a poem might come to you.

But no poem had come because he'd started thinking about arithmetic again, six poems and only three days left, and about how strange it was that all the classes and homework and essays and exams, a whole thirteen years, had cancelled down to this one final assignment, the Writing Folder, Creative Writing 3B. To six pages, the pages that should have held the six poems he couldn't seem to write.

It was like a bad joke. It was weird, so weird it could have come straight from an old fairytale. Write six poems or else! Like the king ordering the miller's daughter, "Weave this straw into gold!"

He'd sat on the swing for ages, thinking of the miller's

daughter and how her father had been so proud of her he'd gone and told the king a lie; he imagined the room she'd been locked up in, piled to the rafters with straw, and how the straw would have covered up the windows so she couldn't see outside.

He hadn't noticed it was getting dark until the little dog had started barking and he'd heard Ms. Brennan call his name. And when he reached home the letter was there after all, and he couldn't believe it for a moment, even though he was holding the thing in his hand, the long white envelope with his parents' names typed neatly across the center, and the crest of Glendale Secondary up there in the corner.

For a few seconds he'd hoped he'd made a mistake and the crest belonged to some other institution, the Council Offices or the Electricity Company or even the Salvation Army. But it was Glendale Secondary all right, and though he'd closed his eyes like a little kid and wished it would disappear—a fairy's gift that vanished when you lied—it stayed there, solid in his hand.

And then Naomi had heard him and come running out into the garden and he'd thrust the letter down into his schoolbag, out of sight. It was still there, hours after dinner, lying in the bottom of his bag. He hadn't given it to them yet.

It wasn't his father's reaction he was worried about; Dad had given up on him long ago. It was Mum. She still believed in him a bit and he couldn't bear to think of her face as she read that letter, the way her eyes would go. They'd go still. Even before she opened it, the moment she saw the school crest, she'd know it was bad news. And she'd act just like he had, clutching at some wild silly hope that the letter was a mistake and meant for someone else.

He'd give it to her tomorrow.

He'd miss the last four weeks of classes, all the exam tips and revision, but he'd still be able to do the exams; he'd checked in the handbook: you could sit them in this place they had in town for kids who didn't have a school.

But what about his Writing Folder? The handbook hadn't said anything about that. Whatever he wrote now would be shit, but he still wanted to hand it in. Would they let him? Would Ms. Brennan be allowed to mark it? He could have asked her in the park, but he hadn't known then. And neither had she; Stringer couldn't have told her he'd been chucked out.

He wasn't going back to school to ask, he was never going near that place again.

Luke raised a hand to his forehead and the hand came away all wet; the sweat was pouring from his skin. And—God, he was *walking*, he'd actually been walking round and round his room and he hadn't even noticed he was doing it. He sat down on his bed and then jumped straight up again; he couldn't seem to keep still.

Like Danny Pearson's cousin Petie.

Petie had been hooked on speed; he couldn't stay still for a second; he'd jump up and walk round, taking things up and putting them down, opening drawers and cupboards and closing them again. He'd change his clothes while you were talking to him in his room, over and over, switching from jeans to shorts and back again to jeans. It made your skin feel itchy just to watch him.

Luke lay down on the bed. And then he sat up again. He had to *know* if he could still hand in the Writing Folder. He had to know *now*; suddenly that seemed the most important thing in the world. He'd ask Caro; Caro always knew things like that.

He jumped up from the bed. He'd ask her now. He couldn't ring because it was too late, past one o'clock already, but he could go over to her house. Caro would probably still be up, she often worked till after one; he'd go round to her window and if the light was out, well, he'd just have to come back home again.

Luke grabbed his jacket from the back of the chair. He bent down to pick up his shoes. Stooping, he saw the schoolbag with the letter hidden inside and the sight of it made him feel strange. It was like being very small and seeing right in front of you the feet and legs of the person who scared you most in the whole world.

In Caro's Room

There was no light in Caro's room. But Luke didn't go away like he'd promised himself, he stayed standing on the path outside her window, as if his feet had grown roots into the ground. And though he thought he hadn't made a sound, Caro's light came on and there she was, peering out at him through the glass.

"Hurry up," she whispered, sliding the window open, grabbing roughly at his arm.

Luke scrambled over the sill. Her room was hot and dazzling, the furniture jumped and wobbled before his eyes. Caro's fingers dug sharply into his arm. "What are you *doing* here?"

"I just wanted to ask you something," he said lamely. "I came round after school but no one answered the door."

"I was in bed," said Caro, "and Mum was at the chemist's." She dabbed at her nose with a crumpled tissue and he saw how her face was puffy and her eyes rimmed angrily with red. She had a cold; that's why the room was hot and smelled of eucalyptus, and why she hadn't been at school. She was sick, and now he'd woken her up.

"Was that you who rang up last night?" she demanded suddenly.

"I'm sorry," he said. "And look, I'm sorry I—"

Caro glared at him. "Dad said it was you. What did you want?"

For a moment, he couldn't actually remember. Last night seemed a very long time ago. "I wanted to say I was sorry," he said at last.

"Sorry?"

"For rushing off—you know, leaving you down there at the station."

Caro frowned. "But why did you ring so late? And why are you here *now*?"

"Now?" he echoed vaguely. Because the funny thing was, he'd almost forgotten the reason, though back in his room, the question of whether he could still hand in his Writing Folder, and where, had been so sharp and urgent in his mind. Now he saw that running over here in the middle of the night, waking Caro up to ask her this, was crazy. Why had he done it?

"Yes, *now*," Caro was saying irritably. "You said you came over to ask me something. What was it?"

His foot caught the edge of an empty Coke bottle and sent it rolling noisily across the floor.

"Shhh! For God's sake, Luke! You'll wake them up! And Dad's really mad at you."

"Sorry."

"Shut up saying sorry all the time! And sit *down*." She almost pushed him into the chair beside the window. "So what was it?" she demanded again.

He certainly wasn't going to ask her that crazy question about the Writing Folder now. He'd tell her about Stringer's letter instead. Was that why he'd really come over, even though he hadn't realized it? He felt all mixed up. "Stringer chucked me out," he said.

"What!" Caro sank down on the bed. "I can't believe it! I can't believe even Stringer would chuck you out for such a little thing. For hanging around in someone's backyard!" She looked at him sharply. "What did he say?"

"He didn't say anything, not to me. He wrote to Mum and Dad."

Caro dragged another tissue from the box beside her pillow. "What did they say? Your mum and dad?"

Luke shifted uneasily in his chair. "I haven't told them yet."

"What? I thought you said Stringer sent them a letter."

"He did. But they haven't got it. I mean, I found it in the mailbox and I haven't given it to them yet."

"Luke! You've got to give them that letter! You can't just hide it, they'll find out anyway." She ran a hand through her tousled hair, exasperated. "How on earth are you going to explain why you're not going to school? And the exams—" Caro broke off; he wasn't even *listening* to her, just sitting there, staring into space.

Luke was listening, but not to Caro. Far away, he could hear the night train coming; its whistle sounded clearly in the stuffy little room. "Hear that?" he asked.

Caro's eyes flew to the door; had her parents woken? But the house was perfectly silent. "What?" she whispered.

"The night train."

"Night train?"

"You know, I told you, the one that comes by really late at night."

"Oh that. Listen, Luke—"

"Didn't you hear it? Just then?"

She shook her head impatiently. "I didn't hear a thing."

That was the second time, thought Luke. Mum hadn't heard it either, last night when they'd been standing outside Naomi's room. And yet it was so *loud*. A frightening idea slid into his mind, a drowned face rising in the water. What if—he pushed the thought away from him.

"Listen, Luke, concentrate, will you? What are you going to do?"

"I'll sort something out."

"Like what? Look, first thing tomorrow, you have to tell your parents, okay? Give them that letter."

"Sure." He smiled at her guiltily, shocked by the tiredness on her face. He shouldn't have come. It would be mean to pester her about the Writing Folder now. He'd stuff it through the letterbox down at the school; if Ms. Brennan wasn't allowed to mark it, she'd send it on wherever it had to go. He blinked dazedly; why hadn't he thought of that before?

"And look, Luke, I think—"

He watched her lips; he felt quite sure she was going to say, "I think we shouldn't see each other for a while." But there wasn't time for her to say anything, because all at once there were footsteps out in the passage and a harsh, hard knocking on the door.

Caro sprang from the bed. "Quick! Out the window!"

"Caroline!" The doorknob rattled.

"It's Dad! Hurry!"

Luke wasn't fast enough. The door burst open and Mr. Hunter came rushing into the room. Luke stumbled to his feet, catching his jacket on the back of the flimsy chair. The chair fell over and Mr. Hunter seized him by the arm. "You little swine!"

"Let him go!" shrieked Caro. "Let him go!"

The shriek startled Mr. Hunter; he dropped Luke's arm and turned to face his daughter.

"Dad, it's not what you think," she said quickly.

"What is it, then?"

"Luke just came over to talk, honestly. He's got a problem at school, that's all."

"Came over to talk? At two o'clock in the morning? Do you think I was born yesterday?" exploded Mr. Hunter. He turned to Luke, pushing his face so close the boy could feel the heat of his skin. "I want you to keep away from my daughter, understand? Keep your hands off her or I'll knock you into the middle of next week!"

"Mr. Hunter, we *were* only talking. I know I shouldn't have come over so late, but—"

"Do you think I don't know what's going on?"

"Dad!"

"What?"

"Shut up! Just shut up!"

"Don't tell me to shut up, you little slut! After what you've been up to tonight!" Mr. Hunter glared at the rumpled bed.

"You've really got sex on the brain, haven't you?" sneered Caro.

"Eh? What did you say?" Mr. Hunter's face flushed darkly.

"You've got sex on the brain, Dad. *You* have, not me, or Luke. Every boy I go out with, every boy I even talk to, all you ever think it is—is sex!" Caro crumpled suddenly and began to cry. Luke took a step towards her but Mr. Hunter pushed him back. "Get out of here!"

Caro looked up. "Yes," she said quickly, "you'd better go now, Luke. Just—go."

"I'm sorry," he whispered, but she didn't even look in his direction.

Luke was halfway down the side path when Mr. Hunter's voice came bellowing out into the night. "Your parents will be hearing from me!"

The Chain of Love

Sometimes when Luke was trying to get to sleep he saw faces. Mostly they were familiar, but sometimes he saw the faces of strangers, people he'd never met in his life. A few nights back he'd seen a lady with a long fair plait dangling down her back; she was opening the door of a tall cupboard and she turned, looking back over her shoulder as if she'd heard someone coming. Once he'd seen a little girl with dandelions in her hair; she'd been so *real*: one flower hung askew, tumbling over her ear, and there'd been a gritty smudge of dirt across her cheek.

The face Luke saw tonight frightened him. It was an ordinary face, a young man in a green peaked cap, staring out through a great wide windscreen where huge wipers swung slowly to and fro. Behind him was a lighted cabin full of dials and switches and levers. It was the expression on the young man's face which scared Luke; the way his eyes stretched wide with terror and astonishment, as if the worst thing in the world was happening right there in front of him and he couldn't do a thing about it.

Luke threw the Doona back; it was useless trying to sleep now, tomorrow was almost here, and he scrambled back into his clothes, even slipping his jacket on because the house seemed suddenly freezing cold. He took the letter from his schoolbag and thrust it into his pocket; he'd give it to Mum today. And today, too, Caro's dad would ring up or even come round to the house.

He went quietly downstairs and into the TV room, closing

the door behind him, switching the set on and turning the sound down low. Singles' ads came flickering onto the screen: why be lonely, a soft sweet voice was asking; why stay at home on Saturday nights when that Very Special Person might be waiting for you on the Chain of Love? When all you had to do was dial this number and add your message to the Chain?

Luke shifted restlessly upon the sofa. Mr. Hunter had thought he'd been in bed with Caro—he wished it was that simple; he wished he was that sort of kid, careless and normal, jumping in through Caro's window because he wanted sex. At least that was something you didn't have to struggle to explain, even to yourself—sex was something anyone could understand.

The ads finished and a documentary began; mothers searching for the bodies of their sons lost in a war somewhere on the other side of the world. It was cold there; you could see it in the blackness of the road, in the grey-smudged patches of snow and the way the skinny leafless trees bent sideways in the wind. The mothers wore bulky coats and furry hats and padded boots which came up to their knees. They clustered round the army guy who'd been assigned to help them, tugging at his sleeve like little kids. He didn't push their hands away. "I have to know," one cried at him, "I have to *know*."

"Tomorrow," the army guy told them, taking a crumpled paper from his pocket. "Tomorrow, I think we shall have news." You could hear in his voice how he didn't think they had a hope, and that he'd been saying "tomorrow" for a long long time.

He was trying though, thought Luke. You could see that in his kind, tired face and the way he was patient with the mothers and didn't get fed up; he was doing his best even though he knew what it said on his piece of paper was useless and the missing sons would never be found. He was trying. He still cared.

And for a second something stirred in Luke, something strange and joyful which was like a promise, if only he could work out what it was. Yeah, even in a really bad place, you could—

And then he noticed the soldier with bored and empty eyes, standing by the roadside, a gun hanging from his shoulder, watching the little group of mothers as if they were things instead of people, no different from the rubble of the ravaged houses or the broken shellcases littering the road.

His face was just like Stringer's.

Luke jumped up and almost ran from the room and down the passage to the telephone. He found Stringer's name in the directory and dialed the number for the Chain of Love. It was all so simple he could hardly believe his luck; he didn't even have to give a credit card number. Luke entered Clyde B. Stringer on the Chain of Love: his name and address, a message and description which would bring that Very Special Person to his doorstep. He made Clyde young and spunky, into leather, bikes, hard rock, and dope, and Clyde was looking for a chick who liked to rage.

What he'd done there was something Stringer would term "a police matter," thought Luke, putting down the phone, but it was worth it for the bikie girl in spikes and leather ringing Stringer's doorbell, her Kawasaki parked outside.

Back in the TV room the mothers in their boots and furry hats had gone, a comedy in bright colors filled the screen. Luke flicked the sound off.

"Luke, what are you doing down here?"

He looked round. His mother was standing in the doorway, hovering anxiously, not quite daring to come in.

"I couldn't get to sleep," he said. "So I came down here."

"But it's so late, dear."

"I know. The night train went through ages back."

He hadn't meant to say that; the words had slipped out, bringing with them the frightening idea he'd had in Caro's room. He pushed it down again; he didn't want to think about that idea, ever.

"What?" his mother was saying, the worry deepening in her eyes.

He *hated* that worry, it made him angry, it made him feel there was something wrong with him. It made him want to shout at her, "Don't *look* like that!"

"What did you say?" she asked again.

"Nothing."

Margaret stood there. She saw her son was wearing his clothes at four o'clock in the morning; he even had his jacket on. Against its deep green color his face was the shade of old paper. He looked dazed.

Just lack of sleep, she told herself. He hardly seemed to sleep at all; sometimes in the middle of the night she'd wake and hear him roaming round the house, along the passages, down the stairs. Last night she was almost sure she'd heard the "ping" of the telephone receiver going down, and tonight she *knew* she had.

Who did he call at this hour? Some classmate who stayed up late to work? She didn't know who his friends were, or even if he had any; it was a long time since he'd brought anyone to the house. A long, long time. How long? Back when he was at St. Crispin's, surely? Almost two years ago, she realized, startled. Two years! She longed to rush across the room and put her arms around him, to ask, straight out, "Darling, what's gone *wrong*? What is it? Tell me!"

He'd flinch away, she knew it; he hated her worrying about him, pestering. Sometimes she found it hard to believe he was the same little boy who'd used to tell her everything. So all she risked was, "Why are you wearing your clothes?"

"I was cold."

"I wish you wouldn't stay up so late."

"I wasn't staying up, I couldn't sleep, I told you."

"You can't go without sleep, darling." He was so thin, Margaret thought, noticing how the green jacket hung in folds from his shoulders; he was like a stick whittled almost into nothing by someone who had no talent with the carver's knife. "Would you like to see a doctor?" she asked.

Luke went perfectly still. It flashed through his mind that Mrs. Lewis might have rung his mother with the suggestion that he see a shrink. Hadn't she said, "That might not be a matter for you to decide"? They could have fixed up everything, he panicked, arranged the appointment without telling him.

"What kind of doctor?" he asked warily.

"What kind? What do you mean?"

"I meant—*what kind of doctor is he?*"

"Well, I don't know. He's just a GP, isn't he? Dr. Franklin?"

Luke relaxed. Just Dr. Franklin. Old Dr. Franklin down at the clinic.

"He might give you a tonic, or something to help you sleep."

"No, it's okay, Mum."

"Are you sure?"

He nodded. "I'll be fine."

"Would you like a cup of tea or something?"

"No thanks."

She looked at him doubtfully; she hovered at the doorway like a poor unhappy ghost whose message can't be heard. "All right. But darling, do go to bed now, please."

"I will," he promised. "In a minute."

He didn't, though. He waited till she'd gone upstairs, till the door of the bedroom closed, then he zipped up his jacket and headed for the back door.

As he passed Molly's room he felt a sudden urge to see her; just *see* her, that was all. He pushed the door open; the light from the hallway shone across the bed. She was sound asleep.

"Hi," he whispered. "Hi, Captain Coolibah."

Unexpectedly, Molly opened her eyes. She raised her head and stared straight at him. Even though her eyes were open Luke could tell she was really still asleep; in the morning she wouldn't even remember seeing him.

"You used to be nice," she grumbled sleepily, and then her eyes closed and her head tumbled back down on the pillow.

Luke shut her door; he left the house through the laundry, hurrying up the path and out the gate into the street.

His feet just started walking.

Riding Through the Clouds

Luke jogged slowly down Orchard Court, past the gates his little sister closed each night to keep him safe, and then turned left along the highway. It was four thirty in the morning and still dark. A fog had rolled in over the city; the trees and houses floated, vanishing and strangely reappearing, like ships on a billowing sea.

He'd gone almost a mile when he heard the dull roar of a tired engine laboring slowly up the hill behind him; he turned and saw two great round lamps of headlights gleaming through the mist, breasting the crest of the rise.

A bus. Luke held up his hand. A bus would take him farther if only it would stop for him. It stopped. The driver's face peered down at him through a lighted windscreen where big wipers swung slowly, and Luke's heart jumped, remembering the face he'd seen so clearly on the edge of sleep. But that had been a young face; the bus driver was old, and instead of a green peaked cap he wore a knitted hat pulled down against the cold.

"Where to?"

Luke hadn't thought of any destination. He didn't know where the bus was going, or where he was going, either. He'd just wanted to get away from the house for a bit, he wanted time to think. "Last stop," he told the driver, reaching into his pocket for a two-dollar coin, taking the flimsy ticket from the machine.

He'd have to hand Stringer's letter over the minute he got home; that was the first thing. Hiding someone else's mail was probably some criminal offense; Stringer would have the official name for it, like he'd had the name for sitting in the Hamiltons' gazebo: trespass.

It had been trespass, when you thought about it in that terse official way, in the language of forms and files and records. He *had* gone wandering into a place where he'd had no right to be. That he'd gone to remember a time when he'd been different was a personal, private thing that didn't count in the real world.

Luke slid into a seat and leaned his face against the cold window: outside the suburbs rolled by silently; in the valleys the mist was thick as clouds; the old bus could have been riding through the sky. The sodium lights shone like beacons or the fiery swords of heroes marching off to save the world.

He'd felt like a hero that day he'd stood up to Gosser on Wood Hill Station, telling him he was sick and twisted because he liked scaring kids and making them scare smaller ones. He'd felt he'd been doing right. But now he wondered if he'd just been silly. Had what happened to that little kid on the train simply been something that went on every day in the world, and no business of his? Could it be true, like Dad said, that the important thing was what went on your record, because that was what people thought you were?

Way back in Grade Four—he must have forgotten his home-work that day—Mrs. Tully had hauled him out to the front of the class together with Alex Hamilton, who must have remembered his. She'd told everyone how he and Alex were both clever boys from nice families, but Alex Hamilton was the kind of boy who'd make a success of his life, while Luke Leman would always be in trouble.

"Don't worry about her," Alex had said in the playground later. "She's just a stupid old witch. She doesn't know a thing."

Luke had thought so himself at the time, but now he wondered if old Mrs. Tully had seen something, if there was something in him that people could actually recognize, like a mark tattooed upon the skin.

Always, even when he'd started failing at school, even when the padlock had snapped shut on his brain, deep down Luke had felt he was clever. He'd believed that one day, when he really put his mind to it, things that seemed so difficult now might become easy, and everything would change, like Ms. Brennan had said.

But Mrs. Lewis hadn't thought so; she'd said he'd still mess up and he'd mess up because that was the kind of person he was.

Had she been right? Had old Mrs. Tully been right? Even Stringer?

The engine of the bus grew deeper, accelerating on a long straight stretch of empty road. They might be right, it thrummed and chanted, they might be right they might be right.

Had he been fooling himself? Had he really been clever when he was in Primary School and later on, at Riversdale? Or had the work just been easy, kiddy stuff that anyone could do? Even his poetry—couldn't that have been some kind of fluke? Because if he'd really been good he'd have been able to do those poems for the Writing Folder. No matter how nervous he was about exams and stuff, he'd have been able to manage if he was any good.

They might be right.

"Where are you off to so early, then?" The bus driver's question made him sound like the wolf in *Red Riding Hood*. Dad used to read that story years ago, when Luke had been so little he hadn't even started school. Dad would act the story out, growling and bounding across the carpet on all fours, leaping onto the sofa, teeth bared in a big grinning snarl. It was like Dad had been another person then, too.

"Eh?" prompted the driver.

"I'm off to visit my grandma."

"Gets up early, does she?"

"Yeah."

Dad had changed because of him. He hurt people, Luke saw suddenly—Dad and Mum, Caro, and even Molly, who thought he was a total idiot now. Ms. Brennan, who'd trusted him and was going to have the shock of her life if she ever got to see that Writing Folder.

"Here we are!"

The bus was drawing to a stop. Luke glanced through the window; they were in the bus station at Eastland Mall. As he got up from the seat his head spun slightly, he was starting to feel tired now. He stumbled going down the steps; they didn't feel solid under his feet.

It was getting light; groups of early workers stood waiting for their buses, muffled up in coats and scarves, stamping their feet to keep warm. The main entrance to the mall was locked and shuttered, but round the side Luke found a small door left open for the cleaners; he slipped through it and wandered down a narrow passage, emerging suddenly into the middle of the plaza.

How strange it seemed at this time of the morning, with all the lights on and water tinkling in the fountain, with dresses and suits and jewelry and perfumes and china shining in the windows and no one around to see! It made you feel like the only person left in the world.

Luke strolled on slowly, his sneakers squishing on the freshly polished floor. He gazed into the window of a Chinese grocery at fat white slabs of bean curd, dried fish, and fragrant sticks of lemon grass, at carved chopsticks and dragon teapots and tiny jars of Tiger Balm. He imagined a little Chinese grandmother in black pajamas buying a pot of Tiger Balm because it reminded her of home.

He passed on to the Estate Agency, pausing to study the photographs in the window, trying to picture the kind of house he might have when he was grown up. He couldn't. An image of Dad's scrapheap flared suddenly inside his head: a huge mountain of rubbish rising to the sky, with kids thrust into it head down, their arms and legs sticking out like stray twigs from a bonfire.

A hand fell heavily onto his shoulder. Luke looked up into the face of a security guard.

"What do you think you're doing, son?"

"Just looking," said Luke. "Looking at the houses."

"Bit early, aren't you?"

"Yeah," Luke agreed, and stood waiting for the guy to tell him what he'd done. Would it be another act of trespass? Intent to steal? Would he get carted off to the cops?

The guard was big and bulky in his hard blue uniform and there was a leather pouch at his belt which might have held a gun. But his face was all right; it was a tired face, with clever kindly eyes. He looked a bit like the army guy on the TV documentary, the one who'd been nice to the mothers. "You kids," he said. "Don't know what to do with yourselves, do you?" He smiled. He could have had a kid Luke's age at home, a kid he liked and talked to in the evenings in front of the TV. "Run along now," he said. "Go home, if you've got a home. It's nearly time for breakfast."

I Didn't Know You Had a Brother

All day in her office, Margaret was haunted by the image of Luke slumped in front of the television at four o'clock in the morning, fully dressed and with his jacket on, as if he was going out somewhere, or had just come in. His pale face stared back from her computer screen, dazed and hollow-eyed. She wondered all over again just where he went those evenings he came home late. And who did he ring up in the middle of the night?

She thought of drugs; drugs would have been an obvious answer to the puzzle of why he failed at school. She'd often studied Luke's bare arms, searching for needle marks; peered at his eyes, uselessly, because she was never able to remember if drugs made the pupils go big or small. She'd gone through his wardrobe, his drawers, the whole of his room. She'd searched through his schoolbag one evening when he was in the shower, creeping like a thief, glancing over her shoulder at every sound, her heart thudding like an engine deep inside her chest.

She'd found nothing. But that didn't make her feel safe.

The phone calls at night, his loss of weight—and it was useless to ask him. If he was on drugs, he'd never tell her, and if he wasn't, her question would be unforgivable.

Margaret finished work at three and picked Naomi up from Kindergarten. The little girl's chatter about her day—Simon Forster spilling paint on Sarah's hair, Kelly Biber screaming at Mrs. Lester, and someone called Bumpty who sounded like a guinea pig but couldn't have been because he talked—almost drove Margaret mad. "Be quiet!" she snapped at poor Naomi, and then had to stop the car and say she was sorry and comfort the little girl.

When they reached the house Luke wasn't there, but then he wouldn't be, Margaret told herself, even if he'd come straight home from school. It was barely three thirty.

Molly was home; St. Catherine's had sport on Friday afternoons. There was a trail of Molly through the house; her schoolbag flung down inside the door for people to trip over, the TV blaring, two muddy school shoes on the sofa, standing guard beside a sticky plate of crumbs.

Margaret followed the trail, picking up and putting right. It led her to the kitchen where she found Molly's blazer thrown carelessly on the table, one rich purple sleeve lying in the butter dish. That blazer had cost the earth! And when she'd reminded Molly of this, three days back, finding it sodden and trampled on the bathroom floor, Molly had rounded on her. The cost of the blazer wasn't her fault, she'd yelled at Margaret; she'd never asked to go to a private school. They could take her out if they wanted to. Her voice had trembled on those last few words, because Molly really loved St. Catherine's.

Margaret gathered the blazer from the table, shaking out the crumbs and creases. She squinted at the greasy cuff: the butter would probably come out, the blazer would be as good as new. You had to look on the bright side, sometimes—at least Molly was doing well at school, at least there was that, she wasn't like her brother.

And then the worry about Luke came flooding back. She hurried from the room blindly, and bumped into Molly rushing down the hall. Before she could stop herself, the question came tumbling from her lips, "Molly, do you know what's wrong with Luke?"

"Wrong?" echoed Molly, her eyes skittering away from her mother's face.

"Yes, *wrong*! Do you know if there's something the matter at school?"

"I don't know anyone who goes to that school," said Molly.

"But has Luke said anything to you?"

"No," said Molly. "Look, Mum, he wouldn't tell me anything; he doesn't talk to me. Naomi's the only one he bothers with round here."

"Yes, but do you know where he goes in the evenings, after school?" With each question, Margaret had moved closer to Molly, crowding her; she didn't realize she was doing it.

"No!" Molly backed against the wall. "How would I know?" But then she added, "He just wanders round."

"Wanders round?"

"Mooches about, you know, like some stupid old dero. I saw him up at the park once, sitting on the swings."

"Was he by himself?" Margaret was thinking of drugs again, dealers lurking in the trees.

" 'Course he was by himself. Listen, Mum, I—"

"He was ringing someone up last night; it was four o'clock in the morning."

Molly's mouth twisted in an odd grimace. "Probably Dial-a-prayer."

Margaret flinched, and then went rushing on again. "He was dressed in his outdoor clothes, and he—"

Molly put her hands up to her ears. "Look! I wish you wouldn't go on at me about Luke. I wish you wouldn't! I just don't *know*." Her voice caught in her throat. "I told you before,

I don't know *anything*." She looked down at the floor. "He's just—hopeless, that's all."

"Hopeless. Do you mean he's on drugs?"

Molly's hands swept down, clenching tightly at her sides. "No I *don't*! Mum, why do you always—"

"But anyone can get on drugs, Molly, anyone. And you just said you didn't know anything about him."

"I know that, at least."

"But sometimes he looks funny. His eyes—"

"He's not on drugs, okay? He's not that kind of person."

"What is it then?"

Molly pushed past her. "I've got to go now, Mum, I'm late."

"Late?" echoed Margaret. Then she saw Molly was dressed up, if you could call it that. She was wearing those old ripped jeans she called her "best," and the new top, the one she wouldn't let Margaret even touch.

"Are you going out?"

"I told you," Molly flung over her shoulder, "I told you I wouldn't be in for dinner tonight, I told you on Tuesday."

Had she? Margaret couldn't remember.

Outside in the street a car hooted.

"Be back by twelve," called Molly, rushing out the door. Slam!

The car hooted twice, greeting Molly's appearance in the street.

Lionel!

Margaret ran to the door and wrenched it open, hurtling down the path and through the gate. She was going to *see* Lionel this time!

The car was parked outside the Tibbetts' house, engine running, the passenger door flung open. Molly was getting in.

The windows were darkly tinted and Margaret couldn't see the driver's face. She ran along the footpath.

And then something amazing happened. The engine died, flicked off, the driver's door flew open, a tall young man got out and came towards her, holding out his hand. He smiled. "I'm Lionel Bersée, Mrs. Leman, I'm so pleased to meet you."

Margaret gaped at him, speechless with surprise. He wasn't what she'd expected at all, there was nothing wrong with him; no tattoos or bikie gear, he wasn't drunk or stoned. And he was only a little older than Molly. He was actually wearing a jacket! He was perfectly presentable, he was—a nice young man. She took his offered hand; she didn't know young people still shook hands.

"Thank you," he was saying. For what? wondered Margaret. Surely not for Molly? And then she saw she had Molly's blazer still draped across her arm. Lionel was taking it from her; he must have thought she'd brought it out for Molly in case the night turned cold. "I'll have her back by twelve," he promised. "No worries."

"Oh no," Margaret protested weakly. "No, I wasn't worried at all."

Lionel slid back inside the driver's seat, the engine started, the car swung gently away from the curb. Margaret thought she caught a glimpse of movement from Molly's side, a wave, but she couldn't quite be sure.

She stood on the footpath in a daze.

Why on earth had Molly hidden him?

Why?

What was going on?

"Mum!" Naomi was swinging on the gate. "Mum, can I ask you something?"

"Of course, darling."

"Promise you won't get mad."

"Of course I won't."

"Where's Lukie?"

"Oh, darling," sighed Margaret, stroking the little girl's hair. "It's only early; it's hardly four o'clock. He's probably down at the library."

They'd parked the car and were walking down towards the shops when Molly saw him out of the corner of her eye.

Luke.

He was on the other side of the street, hands in his pockets, head down, bobbing along with one foot on the curb and one in the gutter, like a little kid. Wandering round, just like she'd told Mum.

Molly averted her eyes, but through the air she could almost feel the swing of her brother's head. He'd seen her. She knew it. Any moment now, any moment, he'd come up and say something stupid. He'd call her Captain Coolibah! She tensed, waiting for the sound of his footsteps, his voice, and she clutched fast to Lionel's hand.

The footsteps didn't come.

She had to look round.

He was standing there, perfectly still, gazing after them. Looking, that's all he was doing. Just looking. Molly averted her eyes again.

He was going to fail the HSC a second time, she was sure of it. And then what was he going to do? She couldn't imagine him doing what other kids did, taking a crummy job for a while, flipping burgers or trundling trolleys, saving some money and bumming round the world. Not now. Not like he was now. He wouldn't be able to get it together. She couldn't picture him in an ordinary job either, working in an office or a bank. She couldn't even imagine him robbing a bank—for all the trouble he got into, Luke was really straight. He'd never make it as a crim.

The only thing she *could* picture was Luke hunched up there in his room doing the HSC all over again, third time round. And over and over. And that was horrible, so horrible for him that Molly turned and sent him a wave. Only a tiny wave. And then she walked on faster, holding even tighter to Lionel's hand.

But now Lionel swung round. "Who's that?"

"No one," muttered Molly.

"He seems like he knows you."

Quite suddenly Molly gave in. She couldn't hide Luke forever. Lionel would meet him somewhere. Mum would see to that. On Sunday, probably. "It's Luke," she said in a small voice. "My brother."

"I didn't know you had a brother." Lionel glanced back again. "He doesn't look much like you."

"No he doesn't," agreed Molly fiercely. "He's not a bit like me!"

And then she felt ashamed. Her cheeks burned. Luke. Hadn't he once been her favorite person? When she was little she'd called him Lukie, like Naomi did.

She dropped Lionel's hand and whirled round to give her brother a great grand wave. "Luke!" she called. "Luke!"

He wasn't there; he'd vanished round the corner out of sight.

"Luke Leman," Lionel was saying thoughtfully. "Hey, isn't that the kid they chucked out of St. Crispin's for telling old Gosser off at the station?"

Molly's eyes widened. "How do you know?"

"My brother went to St. Crispin's. Luke Leman's a kind of legend back there. Gosser was a bastard—really evil." Lionel gazed at the empty space where Luke had stood. He sighed. "You know, I'd like to do something like that one day."

"What? Get chucked out of school?"

"Nope. Stand up to someone like Gosser. No matter what."

Molly beamed at him, she loved him even more for saying this. And she could see he meant it, too. "Just a second," she told him. "I'll be back in a moment." And she rushed up the road to the corner round which Luke had disappeared. She had to *tell* him, tell him how back at St. Crispin's he'd become a *legend*, a hero to kids who'd never met him in their lives.

Molly reached the corner and gazed down the street, searching for Luke's familiar figure. She couldn't see him; she'd missed him, he'd turned another corner down the road.

I Just Have to

Luke came slowly up the front path.

Now he would give Mum the letter.

He'd spent the whole day wandering; somewhere in the middle of that day he'd stood still in a street he didn't recognize. "Mum!" he'd said aloud.

And right there, in front of a cream brick house with striped window blinds and a grey cat sitting on the gatepost staring at him from round yellow eyes, he'd decided what he'd do.

He'd give her the letter when he got home; but first he'd try and tell her everything. He had to, because she still believed in him a little bit and he couldn't bear to see that go.

Everything: how he really had tried with his schoolwork, tried and tried, but he just couldn't do it any more. He'd tell her about the padlock feeling, and why he'd gone to the gazebo and to Caro's place in the middle of the night. He knew it would all sound weird but he wanted her to *know*; he wanted her to know he hadn't done it all on purpose because he didn't give a stuff.

She was on the phone when he came through the door into the hall. Caro's dad! But his mother's voice was so light and cheerful he knew it couldn't be anything to do with him.

"Lukie!" Naomi came running into the hall and seized him by the hand. "Come and see! I want to show you something!"

"What?" He let himself be dragged into the living room, sat down amongst the familiar clutter of Naomi's paper dolls.

"This is for you," she said, thrusting one of her paper cutouts into his hand. He looked down and saw a bright blue sweater. "This is mine, is it?"

She nodded.

"Midnight blue," he said. "Just the right color for me."

"And these are my houses, see? This is Mum and Dad's house."

The pretty thatched cottage with roses round the door was just right for Mum, Luke thought, but Dad should have a tall black tower, all to himself.

"And this is Molly's."

A house like a spaceship, all gleaming curves and flashing silver decks, ready to blast off.

"And this is yours!"

He could hardly bear to look. Dad's scrapheap flared in his mind again, the mountain of rubbish where kids were thrown to burn.

Naomi nudged at him. "Don't you want to see?"

He looked down at the picture in her hand. He saw a white castle with turrets and long pointed windows, green and gold pennants flying bravely from its battlements. A castle in the clouds. He hugged his little sister.

"Thanks," he said. "Thanks for the house, Queenie. It's great."

Footsteps crossed the ceiling; his mother was off the phone now, upstairs, walking down the passage to her room.

Now. He felt in his pocket for the letter, began to get to his feet.

"Where are you going?"

"Just upstairs to talk to Mum. Be back in a minute, Queenie."

The letter had acquired a worn look; the envelope was grubby and there was a deep crease down its center. It looked as if he'd had it for weeks instead of just one day. He went to his room for a moment and tried to clean it up, rubbing at the envelope with a tissue, then flattening the creases out. It would have to do.

"Mum!" he called outside his parents' room, but there was no answer; she'd gone downstairs again. Over on the dressing table the old photographs caught his eye: Naomi as a baby, Molly in her Brownie uniform, the little blond kid on the jetty grinning at the world. "You didn't know shit," Luke told the boy. "That's why you look so happy." He slid the letter into his pocket and hurried downstairs again.

Trouble had broken out in the living room: noisy trouble, the sort that Molly called a whirligig.

"You promised!" Naomi was yelling at Mum. "You promised!"

"Oh, darling, I know I did. But now I've got to go over to Mrs. Richards' place, to help her with Sophie's dress. I promised her too."

"You promised me first!"

"I know, I'm sorry. Look, we'll go tomorrow, okay? I'll take you in the morning."

"I want to go tonight. I want to see it with the lights!"

"What's the matter?" asked Luke, edging round the door.

His mother turned to him; her face was flushed and damp-looking. "Oh, I promised I'd take her to see the model village over at Roselands tonight. But Mary Richards rang; she's in a mess with Sophie's costume for the concert tomorrow and I said I'd go over and help her out. And your father's working late and—"

"That's all right," said Luke. "I can take her. We can get the bus." The letter would have to wait; he needed to get his mother by herself. When she came home, he thought, and if Dad was in bed, that might be the right time.

"Yes!" Naomi beamed at her mother. "I can go with Lukie."

Something unexpected happened. "No, no, you can't," his mother said in a quick panicky voice, and the way she sprang in front of Naomi then, protectively, reminded Luke of a scene from a nature film, a lioness guarding her cub from danger.

From *him*, he realized.

She didn't trust him with Naomi! The pain of it ran right through him, as if a long sharp blade had been thrust inside and drawn out swiftly, leaving behind an empty place that filled with shock. He could hardly believe it.

"Why can't I?" Naomi tugged at her mother's skirt. "Lukie knows how to get there. Why can't I go with him?"

"You just can't." Margaret's face was crimson now, and her eyes avoided Luke's. "I don't want you going out with Luke at night. I don't want you wandering round at all hours, getting lost."

"She wouldn't get lost," said Luke quietly. "Not with me." He reached inside his pocket for the letter, because she might as well have it now. It would be useless trying to explain everything to her. If she believed he couldn't be trusted with Naomi, that he cared so little for his sister he'd let her get lost, then she'd never believe a thing he told her. She'd think he was making the padlock business up as an excuse, or else she'd think he was crazy.

He held the letter out. "What's that?" asked Margaret, but then the doorbell rang violently, and went on ringing, an angry finger jammed against the bell.

Caro's dad for sure.

His mother rushed past him, pushing his outstretched hand aside. He shoved the letter back into his pocket; he'd just leave it on the telephone table, then.

Outside, a furious voice was filling the hallway, but it didn't belong to Mr. Hunter.

"Oh!" gasped Naomi when she heard it. "It's *her*!"

"Her?" echoed Luke. "Who? What's the matter?"

"Just *her*." Naomi ran past him and dived behind the sofa. His mother came into the room with Mrs. Jackson from up the street. "Action Jackson," Luke and Alex Hamilton had called her, because she used to run out yelling whenever their football went bouncing over her fence.

Mrs. Jackson's face was tight with indignation. "… and then she went and did it *again*, Mrs. Leman! And it wasn't as if I hadn't spoken to her about it. Last time I caught her, I said, 'Naomi Leman, if I catch you at these gates again, you'll be in trouble!' "

"Where's Naomi?" Margaret asked Luke.

He shook his head, but they all heard the stifled whimper from behind the sofa, and saw the small foot in its bright red sneaker sticking out from the side.

"Naomi, come out from there this minute!"

Naomi crawled from behind the sofa and dashed towards Luke.

"Come here!" Margaret grabbed her arm as she rushed past. "Naomi, have you been going out in the street by yourself? At night, after all I told you?"

"Not at night," whispered Naomi. "Not when it's really dark. Just when it's *starting* to get dark."

Margaret shook the little girl's arm. "How many times have I told you not to go out by yourself at night? Or at any other time? And why have you been shutting Mrs. Jackson's gates? *Have* you been shutting them when she told you not to? Is that true, Naomi?"

Mrs. Jackson's eyes flashed angrily. "Of course it's true. And it's not just our gates; it's everybody's gates. I've seen her out there time and time again. *Up* the street she goes, and *down* the street she goes, shutting all the gates."

"Is that true, Naomi?"

"Yes," muttered Naomi, her face hidden in her mother's skirt.

"Why?"

"Because I *have* to." Naomi's voice was muffled.

"You have to? Why? Why on earth do you have to shut people's gates?"

"Probably a dare," suggested Luke. "You know, from one of the kids at Kinder. It was a dare, wasn't it, Queenie?"

"Luke, will you let Naomi answer, please? Naomi?"

Naomi came out from her mother's skirt. Her face was like a small round moon. High on her cheekbones two bright red patches flared. "Because if I don't—" she broke off, catching her bottom lip between her teeth.

"If you don't, what?"

"Nothing!" Naomi shouted. "I just have to, that's all. I HAVE TO SHUT THE GATES!" She dragged free from her mother's hand and charged across the room. "I hate you!" she roared as she fled past Mrs. Jackson. "I hate you I hate you I hate you!"

"Well!" gasped Mrs. Jackson.

They stood there in silence, listening to Naomi's footsteps running up the stairs and down the passage to her room. A door slammed violently.

"Well!" said Mrs. Jackson again. She licked her lips. "Little madam!" she declared.

The Walls Are Thin

"I couldn't seem to get through to her. She wouldn't give me any reasons!" Sitting up in bed, her arms clasped round her knees, Margaret was telling Dan about Naomi. "She just kept on saying, 'I have to,' all the time."

Dan Leman stood in the middle of the room, carefully fastening the buttons of his blue pajama jacket, concentrating on them, button by tiny button, wishing he was far away and didn't have to hear all this.

"Why on earth would she do such a thing?" Margaret asked him. "Why?"

Dan wanted to put his hands over his ears, but he knew he had to listen, even try and find an answer. He didn't have any answers; he felt, at this moment, that he didn't know anything. "Little kids can be funny sometimes," he mumbled.

"Not Naomi. She's always been such a nice child, you know that. Sunny—a sunny child. Honestly, Dan, the way she stood there and defied me! I could hardly believe my ears! And the way she spoke to Mrs. Jackson!"

"That old trout!"

"Yes, but that's not the point, Dan. It's Naomi—she seemed like another child, like she'd been bewitched or something!"

Dan got into bed. He lay down but Margaret kept on sitting up, going on and on about Naomi. With some sure instinct he knew at any moment she was going to switch to Luke; he would have to hear about Luke tonight. Once, through the thin walls of a holiday hotel, he'd heard two little kids crying to their parents,

"You only had us to torture us!" The boot was on the other foot, he thought.

"I can't help thinking—" Margaret began haltingly.

"Can't help thinking what?" asked Dan, and sighed.

"Well, that Luke—" she said the name defiantly, with a quick glance in Dan's direction "—that Luke might have had something to do with it."

There. Dan played dead, like a big uneasy animal beneath the Doona.

"That it was some silly game, some idea he put into her head," Margaret went on. "She's the only one he really talks to, did you realize that? And the other night I found him outside her room; he said she'd had a nightmare and he was getting her back to sleep, but oh! I don't know."

Dan lay there without a word, his head turned away from her, sideways on the pillow, as if he thought he could escape that way. And then he felt a slap, a little one, but still a slap, on his arm, through the thin stuff of his pajama sleeve. His eyes jerked open; he turned his head.

Margaret was glaring down at him. "Just stop doing that!" she said angrily.

"Doing what?" Dan rubbed at his arm.

"Pretending. Stop pretending, stop trying to hide!"

"Hide?"

"From Luke. Ignoring Luke. Never talking to him. Never talking about him, never letting *me* talk about him!"

"I do let you talk about him."

"No you don't. You run away. You pretend he doesn't exist." She drew in a long, shaky breath. "It's horrible, the way you just walk past him. I can't bear to see it. Your own son. It's—cruel."

"He—" began Dan, but before he could get out another word,

Margaret clamped a hand over his mouth. "Don't say that, don't say it!"

Dan pushed her hand away. "Say what?"

"'He's on his own now.' I hate it when you say that."

"I wasn't going to," Dan protested sulkily. He heaved himself up from the pillow and put his arm round his wife's shoulders.

"Oh, I'm so worried about him, Dan," she burst out. "I don't know where he goes or what he does; I don't know whether he's working or not, shut up in his room for hours. I'm afraid he's just lying there, Dan; I'm afraid to look in and see." She drew another long breath, so deep and violent it fluttered the ends of her hair. "Oh, there's never a moment's peace with him; it's always things going wrong, over and over again. And when I look back, do you know—sometimes I can't seem to remember one single happy thing? With Luke." Her voice bounced out against the thin white walls and echoed round the room. "That can't be true, can it, Dan? That can't be true?"

"No," he whispered. "It isn't true."

"There's something wrong with him! I *know* there is!"

"Shhh," he whispered. "Shhh, Margaret."

They sat there in silence for a moment, and then Dan said in a low confused voice, "It might be something to do with us. What's wrong with Luke, I mean."

Margaret looked into his face, astonished that he, of all people, should say this. "With us? How?"

He shook his head slowly. "I don't know. I just keep thinking it might be—somehow." He took his arm from Margaret's shoulders and began to get up from the bed.

"What are you doing? Where are you going?"

"Just to have a word with him." He saw the alarm in her eyes. "What is it? I thought you wanted me to talk to him. All this time—"

"Oh yes, yes, I do. But don't get angry with him, Dan. Don't start fighting."

"I won't," he said.

Dan didn't have far to go; Luke's room was next to theirs. He stood outside the door. Now that he was here he didn't know what he was going to say. It was months since he'd spoken to the boy, and now suddenly that punishing silence seemed stupid to him, and cruel, like Margaret had said. How could he have done such a thing? He'd behaved like a sulky child, like a kid who'd opened a Christmas present and found the wrong gift inside.

"Luke," he called shyly and when there was no answer he pushed the door open and looked inside. Luke was asleep; a long still hump beneath the eiderdown.

"What happened?" Margaret was waiting for him, still sitting up in bed, her eyes fixed on the door.

"Nothing. He was asleep. I'll talk to him in the morning." Dan got into bed and switched off the light. He went to sleep.

Margaret stayed awake. She thought of Luke when he was a little boy; she remembered how once she'd gone into his room to look for something in the wardrobe, and right in the back she'd found an old cardboard box. She'd taken the lid off; the box was full of bread; crammed with crusts and ends of loaves and even moldy sandwiches. "What's this?" she'd asked him.

"It's bread."

"Yes, I can see that, darling. But why is it here? What's it doing in your wardrobe? What are you keeping it for?"

He wouldn't answer her; he'd thrust his fist into his mouth and stared down at the floor. She'd knelt beside him and gently removed the fist. "Why is the bread there, darling? You can tell me."

"It's for the war," he'd whispered.

"War?" She'd been shocked; he was four. She hadn't realized he'd even known the word. "What war, darling?"

"The war with bombs," he'd said. "That war. On the TV. So when it comes here, we'll have something to eat."

She saw his small white face again, turned up to her, white and pinched with the terrible secret he'd been carrying round inside him. Dazed.

Just like he'd looked last night, she thought.

Like Naomi had looked this evening.

The Night Train

Luke hadn't been asleep.

The walls were thin. He hadn't been able to catch his father's words because Dad's voice had been too low, but he'd heard what his mother said.

"Not one single happy thing!"—that's what she'd said. He'd been wrong about her; he'd known it the moment he saw how she didn't trust him with Naomi.

When his father came up the passage and called to him through the door, Luke had pretended to be asleep. He didn't want to talk to him. Or her.

"Not one single happy thing."

Something snapped in Luke then, you could almost hear it go. And the idea he'd had in Caro's room now stepped out boldly, like a thing that waits in a house for the click of a gate and parents' footsteps fading down the road.

The idea was this: the night train wasn't real.

Its whistle had sounded clearly in Caro's room, and the night before when he'd been standing with Mum outside Naomi's room.

But Mum and Caro hadn't heard it. They hadn't heard a thing.

They hadn't heard it because there weren't any trains after midnight. They hadn't heard it because it *wasn't there*. He was the only one who heard the night train because it was in his head, like the voices of angels and devils Jennifer Brady had heard.

There was something wrong with him. Hadn't Mum just said so, in the room next door? Mrs. Lewis thought so, didn't she? Even Ms. Brennan might think so, though she'd hidden it like Mum had done. And they didn't mean wrong like failing exams or getting chucked out of schools, nothing so ordinary as that. They meant wrong in the head. Crazy.

They might be right.

He switched on the light and grabbed his clothes from the chair. He had to be sure about this, he had to *see*. Because they could be wrong, too, and if there *was* a night train then they were wrong; it was as simple as that.

When you needed the answer to something important, people left you hanging, like Stringer and Mrs. Lewis had done when he'd asked if he'd be expelled. They'd never answer "yes" or "no" straight out. But this answer he could find out for himself.

He reached under the desk for his runners. The socks weren't there. Where were his socks? He got down and peered beneath the desk and under the bed, but he couldn't see them. It didn't matter; all that mattered was to get down to the station and see the night train coming by. *If* it came by.

And if it did, he was all right. He could bear anything as long as he was all right, he could start all over again, somehow, right from the bottom, no matter what people thought of him, no matter if he failed the exams again. He thought of the kind face of that guy he'd seen on the documentary last night, the one who'd been helping the mums who'd lost their sons. That was what you did—somehow—you kept on trying and you stayed kind.

He laced the runners over his bare instep and then up his ankles, tying them in a knot so they wouldn't come loose when he ran. He looked at his watch. It was earlier than he'd thought, only half past twelve, too soon to leave. He lay on his bed and waited. When another hour had passed he got up and left the room.

Outside in the passage he paused outside Naomi's door. She'd gone to bed miserable because Mum had been mad at her, and even when Mum had gone to Mrs. Richards' place Naomi wouldn't come downstairs. He'd taken her some chocolate milk and a piece of cake but she still wouldn't tell him why she'd closed those gates.

He pushed her door open. She'd left the curtains wide again; the faint light shining through the window showed him she was fast asleep. Luke closed the curtains and then tiptoed to the chest of drawers. From the small glass bowl beside the china cats he took four gold sticky stars. He wanted to do something nice for her, something to make her laugh. Gently, kneeling down beside the bed, he pasted the stars in a row across Naomi's forehead. Queen of the Stars! he thought, getting to his feet again, smiling down at her. She'd find them in the morning, see them in the bathroom mirror when she went to clean her teeth. She'd be rapt.

Downstairs, he tossed the letter from Stringer onto the telephone table, beside the electricity bill and the statement from the bank.

Luke had never opened the letter. His mother would open it on Tuesday, four days from now. Inside she'd find an invitation to the Year 12 Parents' Dinner. Just an invitation, but on Tuesday when she found it Margaret would sit down and cry.

The station was closed, locked up. Luke shrugged and turned away; he didn't need a ticket, he wasn't planning on a ride. He just wanted to *see* the train. He crossed the empty car park, walked down the narrow lane behind the railway cottages, and then climbed the grassy slope onto the tracks. He looked down the line towards the city; there was nothing down there, no sign of the train, no tiny pinprick of light coming closer through the dark. To the left at the bottom of the slope the houses and telegraph poles of Harlow Street were so black and sharp they might have been cut out of tin; on his right a line of whispering fir trees hid the secret slopes and hollows of the golf course. Above his head the stars wheeled slowly in a shining sky; the rain had gone, tomorrow would be fine.

His watch said almost two, and there was no sign of the train. Could he have got the direction wrong? Could the night train come the other way, towards the city? Luke swung round, but there was no sign of anything up there either, only the moony glimmer of the locked-up railway station. He curbed the little rush of panic in his blood; the train was late, that was all. Trains were always late, even a night train might be late. It could come at ten past two, he told himself, or even two twenty. He wasn't giving up on it just yet.

He walked on a little, his back to the city now, stepping carefully from sleeper to sleeper like a child playing skip the cracks, avoiding the craggy blue metal in between. A tiny sharp stone lodged in his sneaker, cutting painfully into his foot. Luke balanced on one leg and tugged at the shoe. It was hard to shift because he'd knotted the lace; he tugged and tugged, wobbling one-legged in the middle of the tracks. The laces stretched and the sneaker came free from his foot, but the knot still held it to his ankle.

All at once a wild wind rose, gusting out of the north, tearing at the trees beside the line. Down in Harlow Street a sheet of iron banged and clattered, up in the sky the stars rocked about. The tall firs threshed sideways, beating at the dark. Their roaring filled Luke's ears; it sounds like surf, he thought, still tugging at his shoe. It sounds like the sea.

A brightness like a searchlight flooded over him, a long whistle ripped across the wind. He swung round, treading the sneaker clumsily underfoot, stumbling.

And there it was above him: the night train, the 1:30 postal van from the city. He saw the brilliant lighted cabin, the curved windscreen with the big wipers, the young driver's face a jerk of terror beneath his green peaked cap. It was real. The night train was real. So they hadn't been right. *He'd* been right. So now he could—

Luke staggered and went down. The brakes screamed and the wind roared and there was a strange flat thump like a sack of flour thrown out onto the road.

Luke heard that thump. They always said it didn't hurt, the blow that smashed you up for good, that made your soul come flying out—but it did hurt, it did.

"No!" he heard a voice say somewhere and he saw Naomi standing in a darkened street, her hand on the latch of someone's gate. The wind blew and a shadow fell across her fingers like a mark. He felt himself rise and then fall again as if on the crest of a mighty wave, sucked under into a darkness which filled his mouth, his ears and nose, his eyes.

Back in the house at Orchard Court, Naomi woke suddenly with a small sharp cry. She jerked up straight in her bed, her fingers gripping at the edge of the Doona.

She'd remembered something. She'd remembered how Mrs. Jackson had come to the house and told on her. Naomi screamed. Because now she would never be able to close all the gates again, ever—and now something bad would happen to Lukie.

A Legend

Though it was fine on Saturday, sparkling bright, Liz didn't have her barbecue.

Caro stayed in her room all day. She sat in the chair where Luke had sat on Thursday night. She kept her back very straight; she kept remembering Luke saying "sorry," and how she'd said, "Shut up saying sorry all the time."

Shut up shut up shut up.

Molly passed her parents' room and heard them talking inside, asking each other if Luke's death had really been an accident or if he'd meant to do it.

"He didn't!" she shouted, rushing into the room. "He didn't! He didn't! He didn't!" her shouts growing louder, a ringing noise inside her ears. She fell silent, waiting for the ringing to stop, and the echoing of her voice around the room. "He wasn't that kind of person," she told her mum and dad, who sat staring at her with newborn looks upon their faces, like small birds peeping over the edge of their nest into the scary world. Baby birds who didn't know a thing, thought Molly, and she was about to shout, "You didn't know a thing!" when the sight of those poor faces stopped her and instead she said gently, "Luke was a legend back at St. Crispin's. A *good* legend."

Mary Richards took Naomi to her daughter's concert, and sat holding the little girl's hand, while on stage Sophie danced in the pink dress Margaret had helped to sew on Friday night. Mary thought it was wrong how Naomi hadn't been told about Luke. Not properly. She decided that if Naomi turned to her and asked, she wouldn't keep it from the child.

But Naomi didn't turn, she didn't speak at all, she sat stiffly with her eyes fixed straight ahead, a little frown between her brows, watching Sophie dancing.

On Sunday afternoon three skinny Year 7s went to the railway track to look for blood and signs. Death wasn't real to them. They giggled and snorted and jostled and called out, but each had a funny scared lonely feeling he didn't tell about.

They found nothing. The narrow rails glittered in the sunlight, the tall fir trees stirred and whispered, over on the golf course the Sunday players called to each other: "Bit of a fluke, that, Bob!" and, "Bad luck, you're in the rough!"

It was all just ordinary; that was the scary thing.

"Let's go!" hissed one of the Year 7 kids, and suddenly they all started running, stumbling and scrambling down the grassy slope, racing down Harlow Street, legs pumping, elbows out, hearts thumping wildly in their scrawny chests. They reached the corner and without looking round they scattered, each in his own direction, heading straight for home.

Judith Clarke was born in Sydney, Australia, and educated at the University of New South Wales and at the Australian National University in Canberra. A major force in young adult fiction both in Australia and internationally, she worked as a teacher, librarian, and creative-writing lecturer before beginning to write full-time. She is the author of many award-winning books for young adults, including *Starry Nights*, *Wolf on the Fold*, and *Kalpana's Dream*, which was named a Boston Globe–Horn Book Honor Book. Her most recent novel, *One Whole and Perfect Day*, was published in the United States in 2006. Ms. Clarke currently resides in Melbourne, Australia.